ONLY ECHOES REMAIN

Books by Dody Myers

THE GREATEST OF THESE IS LOVE

THE REBERTS OF LITTLESTOWN

ECHOES OF THE FALLING SPRING

FREDERICA SUMMER

ECHOES FROM THE MIST

TO LOVE AGAIN

ONLY ECHOES REMAIN

DODY MYERS

ONLY ECHOES REMAIN
ISBN 978-1-62268-022-1

Copyright © 2013 by Dody Myers

First printed March 2013

Library of Congress Control Number: 2013934744

Also available as e-book: ISBN 978-1-62268-035-1

Printed in the United States of America on acid-free paper.

Cover design by Craig Faris – www.craigfaris.com

BellaRosaBooks and logo are trademarks of Bella Rosa Books.

10   9   8   7   6   5   4   3   2   1

Part One

1882

Chapter One

August 23, 1882 was a scorcher—ninety-two degrees in the shade by midmorning, air like a sodden blanket. On St. Simons Island lumber men worked in undershirts, business men loosened their collars and fanned themselves with wide-brimmed straw hats, and women in long bathing costumes led children into the sparkling foam of the ocean off the Georgia coast. Clam diggers strolled by with buckets full of quahogs and littlenecks. A pair of sandpipers skittered along the incoming tide so fast their little stick legs left only scratch marks on the hard sand. On the beach a young man and a girl walked hand in hand at the edge of the surf. Calm surf, belying surf that within hours would become a roaring monster. The girl, Amanda Kennedy, was nineteen, short, with blue eyes, and a softly rounded chin often thrust out in defiance. Today her hair, a rich chestnut, was gathered and tied at the nape of her neck to keep it from flying in her eyes. She was from Pennsylvania, a Junior at Wilson College in Chambersburg. She was visiting the boy with her aunt and uncle during summer break. The boy, Michael McKenzie, lived on the island. He was twenty-one, his sun-bronzed skin and high cheek bones hinting at his Native American heritage. He had a strangely sweet grin that was at odds with strong Lincolnesque features.

Amanda and Michael picked their way over small, broken shells and jellyfish on sand that was damp and rippled from the tide. They strolled slowly toward the lighthouse which guarded the southern tip of the island and guided high-masted ships through the channel that separated St. Simons from Jekyll Island. As they walked Amanda noted the numerous summer cottages that had sprung up along the beach, a fact that boded well for Michael who was building a resort hotel on his step-father's former plantation. Dune grass swayed in a sudden gust of welcome wind. They walked along the edge of the incoming tide and Amanda threw back her head and laughed as they jumped to avoid the long rolling swells rising from the ocean bed. Cirrus clouds braided a pale sky, the tang of salt wafted on the air, the wind began to quicken, and the sun hung like a copper globe over a sea turned glassy. Occasionally shrimp fishermen shouted from boat to boat or the lighthouse horn sounded its mournful call. But, overall, there was eerie stillness. No gulls or shorebirds were to be heard. Old timers nodded their heads; animals were always the first to sense a disturbance in the weather.

Michael pulled out his gold pocket watch and flipped it open. "It's getting late," he said. "Maybe we should turn back. My father said he would like to leave for Savannah before noon. Grandma is expecting you for dinner tonight."

"Are you certain you can't join us? We've had such a short time together," Amanda said. Her dark hair loosened in the stiffening wind.

"Dang it all, Amanda, I just can't. They are going to deliver the hotel rugs today and I must be here to make sure they're the ones I ordered." Michael's shoulder-length hair snapped in a sudden gust of wind and he pushed it back. "Crazy weather," he muttered, glancing out to a quickening sea where white caps were beginning to appear and a boat zipped along, sails billowing.

This stretch of the beach was almost deserted and Michael put his arm around her waist. She felt lightheaded—free as the sun and wind, free as a child. She turned to look at his bold profile. He stopped walking and pulled her to him. They kissed. His hand slid down her back and she felt a flash of heat so intense it rocked her.

"Stop Michael. People will see us," Amanda said with mock firmness, pushing him away, fighting to hide a coy smile.

"Not on this beach, they won't." He laughed and pulled her back into his arms. Since he was taller than Amanda by a head, her face nestled comfortably against his chest.

"Um," she murmured. "You smell good . . . like sunshine and salt."

He drew himself up to his full height, while a look of stern pride settled on his face. They stood that way for several minutes, then he took her hand and guided her to a pair of wooden steps leading from the boardwalk down to the beach. They were barefoot, the soft sand beyond the tide line griddle-hot. "Let's sit here for a while," he suggested. He brushed sand from one of the steps and Amanda hiked up her long skirt and slowly sat down.

"Lord, is it always this hot?" she asked with a helpless gesture, fanning herself with her hand.

Michael grinned. "Sometimes it's hotter."

"Don't you miss the change of seasons? I would miss that more than anything."

"Well, on the coast of Georgia and the sea islands of the Carolinas, we do get a sort of seasonal change; but our seasons are different from fall and winter in the north. The change is more subtle. The weather stays warm but not hot. The sea and sky turn a deeper blue, the sun more golden, the marshes turn tawny and luminous. It's beautiful in its own way."

They sat side by side, shoulders touching, watching a sun-tinted sea caress the shore. Michael's strong fingers squeezed hers. The odd light slanting across his high cheekbones was incandescent and arresting. He was striking. The slant of sun showed bronze skin tanned golden, dark eyes under strong brows black as licorice. His hair was black and shiny, along with

his beard which was new and tidy. She wouldn't call him handsome, but then she knew that she was not beautiful. She was
plain with plump arms and legs, her only exceptional features,
thick-lashed, blue-violet eyes. Michael was an extrovert while
she was somewhat of a loner. Her desire for education, coupled
with her terrible feeling of inferiority due to her birth, set her
apart from others. Her eyes stung and filled with tears as she
remembered.

She was seven when she first heard the word *bastard*. She
had run home from school sobbing and burst into the kitchen
where Ila, their cook, was stirring cake batter. "What does
bastard mean?" Amanda asked, her eyes brimming with tears.
"Some fat boy at school said I was a bastard and couldn't play
with them."

"Thet not a nice word," Ila said as she increased the rhythm
of her spoon against the crockery bowl. "Lawd, chile, I thinks o'
you more like the gift of an angel from heaven. Ask yo' mama.
It gots more to do with you daddy than you."

But her mother pushed her questions aside. Somehow, even
then, Amanda didn't think her mother thought of her as a welcome gift. No one ever spoke of her father. Now that she was
older, she knew why.

Michael looked at her with a lopsided grin. A smile crinkled
the skin around his dark eyes and made her heart leap as it had
since they were children and he had come north to live with
Uncle Ford and Aunt Abby.

"I think we should get married as soon as the hotel opens," he
said. "I miss you and want you with me."

"We made an agreement, you know," she reminded him.
Amanda caressed his fingers one by one as she talked. "You
promised I could finish college."

"Yes, I know. But I'm terribly lonely and in addition to being
an excellent hostess you will make a fine wife and mother."

Amanda frowned, her lower lip caught between her front

teeth. *Hostess? Wife and mother? Is that all her education would equip her for?* She didn't quite care for his choice of words. If Michael had a fault, it was his old-fashioned view of women.

He had traveled south two years ago and found his step-father's old plantation home in ruins from the Civil War. A dream was born. He would not return to Pennsylvania to continue his college education, instead he would stay at St. Simons, rebuild the plantation home into a resort hotel and run it as a family business. Sometime in the near future he and Amanda would marry and start a family. He had it all figured out.

Amanda felt a butterfly of unease in the pit of her stomach.

Michael kept his gaze on the sea as he lifted a fold of her blue skirt and slipped his fingers onto her knee. With his other hand he rubbed his new beard and pretended nonchalance. Amanda fought to hide a smile. She witnessed a light pattern of red spread its way across his cheeks and beads of sweat on his lip that she suspected did not come from the sun.

They sat a while longer. "We should say good-bye here," he said. "Everyone will be watching back at the hotel."

"It won't be for long this time," Amanda said. "The whole family is planning to come down in October for the grand opening. The college has agreed to let me off for the entire week. Then too, my mother has arranged to get time off from work and she is taking Erin and Eliza out of school."

She jumped up and lifted her long skirt to shake away the sand. "We'll get married . . . but only after I graduate. You promised." She pulled him to his feet. "Come on, now, slow-poke. I'm not too grown up to race you home."

That afternoon the tears that Amanda had fought to contain when she kissed Michael good-bye streamed down her cheeks. She climbed into the carriage with her aunt and uncle for the trip across the island to catch the ferry to the mainland. They planned to visit Ford's mother in Savannah for two days, then return home to Pennsylvania. Aunt Abby put her arms around Amanda and hugged her. "I know it's hard, dear, but the time will go quickly," she said.

"I feel so guilty, Aunt Abby. Michael wants to get married now and I want to finish college." Her chin lifted in an arc of decisiveness. "I do love him. I'm just not ready."

"And neither is he, if he would only admit it. Getting a new hotel up and running is a huge undertaking. I imagine it will be several years before it provides him a living."

"And then some," Ford interjected from the front seat. He glanced up at the sky. "I think we are getting out of here just in time. A storm's coming. And the island is no place to be in a northeastern blow."

Ford was right. Building on a barrier beach is toying with nature. It is on borrowed land, on a loan from the sea. St. Simons is a spit of land separated from mainland Brunswick on the west by an extensive system of salt marshes and sounds and on the east by the mighty Atlantic. It is the largest of the barrier islands along Georgia's coast—shaped and constantly changed by pounding surf and ocean winds.

But St. Simons had a romantic history and Amanda was slowly falling in love with the charming island. During the 18th century it served as the sometimes home for John and Charles Wesley, chaplains at Fort Frederica and founder of the Methodist Church in America. Fort Frederica, on the northern tip of the island, was the military headquarters for General Oglethorpe during the early colonial period and served as a buffer against Spanish incursions from Florida. During the early 1800s the island was cultivated by English colonists for rice and cotton. The plantations were worked by large populations of African slaves, then destroyed and burned during the Civil War. In the years following the war the coastal islands were in critical condition. Many plantations had been destroyed and the owners suffered financial ruin. Now it was struggling to find a new identity. In 1874 Norman Dodge and Titus Meigs, two million-aires from New York City, decided to start a lumber mill on St. Simons and bought the plantation of James Hamilton Cooper on the Frederica River at Gascoigne Bluff. At present there were four mills operating for which the lumber was cut "up country" and floated on rafts down the Satilla and Altamaha Rivers. Two thousand southern live oak trees had been harvested on St. Simons to build the *USS Constitution* better known as "Old Ironsides." The Dodge, Meigs Mills were very successful and in 1878 they supplied the oak for the roadbed of New York's Brooklyn Bridge.

The era of long-stem cotton and elegant plantation life was gone, replaced by lumber and the emergence of a tourist Indus-try. Ships came to the island from England, South America, and Maine, and their ballast was unloaded on the Mackay River. The Captains of the vessels often brought their wives and children with them to enjoy the wide sand beaches and they began to buy the seaside cottages. Now, tourism was making its debut. People from Atlanta had discovered the island for vacations and it was an excellent stopping point for travelers on their way to and from Florida.

Because the island lay in a curve of the coast line, well east of the gulf stream, hurricanes were practically nonexistent. Still, it was a barrier island and the term "barrier" refers to the protective role the islands and their marshes play in shielding the mainland from oceanic storms. But on this weekend it was to fail miserably in its prescribed role.

•   •   •

Amanda had been gone for only an hour and Michael missed her already. He left his lunch half-eaten, crossed through the main dining room, and stepped out the French doors to the veranda extending along the front of the hotel facing the sea. His brow puckered as he gazed at the turbulent water. He was concerned, but not yet alarmed. The incoming tide was unusually high and should have turned by now. Exceptionally long ocean swells were flattening the dunes. A gale force wind had begun blowing hard from the north to the east and as soon as his parents and Amanda had left for Savannah it began to rain. He felt a slight quiver of uneasiness when a sharp gust whipped his jacket open and tore at his long black hair. The sudden shift in weather confused him, the day felt heavy, the sea a sulky gray, the sky a strange greenish-yellow. He knew he had better secure the hotel boat before things got worse.

Michael ran down to the landing. Braving the hammering rain he backed the boat away from the dock and rowed toward a large cedar tree growing on the bank. He dropped the anchor into its massive roots—they would hold better than sand. Moving quickly he rowed back to the dock, trailing the anchor line behind him. He picked up the bow line and secured it to the boat then rowed back to a place halfway between the tree and the dock where he tied it off *Indian fashion,* like a hammock, clear of any objects that could cause damage.

Satisfied that the boat was safe he returned to the hotel to finish lunch. As he drained his coffee, the mantle clock chimed the hour. The hands of the clock showed that the tide should have turned an hour ago. Alarmed now, he pushed his chair aside, rushed over to the windows facing east and peered through the streaming glass. By this time the sea had risen to the lower part of the landscaped terrace threatening the newly planted heirloom roses. On the section of the veranda encircling the front of the hotel the keening wind had ripped out the wisteria vine and toppled the trellis. In the distance he saw his foreman, James, slinging mud with a shovel beside the drainage ditch bordering the north field. He was apparently not making any headway trying to divert the incoming tide.

Michael ran out to the kitchen pantry, snagged a rain slicker from a peg on the wall and rushed into the yard. He hit the sodden front lawn running, his boots sinking into the soaked turf as he squelched through the mud to help his servant.

Sweat and rain made rivulets on James's black face. "Masta Michael, that tide ain't turned. Water's running up the ditch fast as it should be runnin' out. It blowin' up a hurricane that be for sure."

"Hurricane" was like a foreign word to Michael, a Northerner since a child. He had only read of the tropical storms and certainly never experienced one. His stomach churned. *Oh, God, not a hurricane. Not now. They were booked solid for the opening in October.* By now the water was over most of the yard and still rising. "Better round up the chickens and get them into the stable," he yelled into the howling wind. "I'll help."

In the barn the agitated horses were snorting and pacing in their stalls and several squabbling wild turkeys had banded together in a dark corner. He and James chased the chickens inside, filled the feed buckets with extra oats, and tried to calm the skittish horses. Rain pelted the tin roof and crept under the door. He fed a carrot to his stallion, Hobie, and on impulse kissed his muzzle. "Everything's going to be fine," he whispered. "It's just a bad rain storm." But by now Michael knew it was more than that. What he didn't know was that most hurricanes attack with three weapons: swirling winds, heavy rain, and waves so high that at first glance they may look like a fogbank. This storm had all three.

Up until this time, although blowing a brisk gale, the wind was not causing any major damage. Now each gust became more frequent and seemed stronger than the preceding gust. The sea had begun to churn and the tide still had not turned. Water slithered up the beach and seawall, gathering into pools where Michael had never seen it before.

"I think that's all we can do for now," Michael yelled into the wind. "Better get inside before this gets worse."

A stray chicken ran ahead of him and he drove it onto the kitchen porch. Surprisingly the chicken obeyed and a memory came over Michael of Penelope, Amanda's pet chicken, who used to follow him everywhere. *Please*, he prayed, *let my family be north of this storm.*

He went into the hotel and changed into dry clothing while James' wife, Matilda, ground some coffee beans and brewed a pot of coffee. Carrying a steaming mug of the fresh brew in his cold hands Michael opened the kitchen door and stepped out onto the side porch. He gasped when he saw how far the water had advanced onto the yard. It would soon cover the steps. Matilda appeared at his side and he heard her groan.

"Lawd a mercy, looka that. I thinks it be a good idea to take bread and food from the storeroom to one o' the upstairs bedrooms 'case that water keep a comin."

"It is past time for high water. The tide will surely turn now."

"Tell that to them poor little critters huddlin' on our porch," Matilda muttered, pointing to several pigs, two peacocks, and a groundhog whose home was undoubtedly under water.

Matilda is probably right, Michael thought, his stomach tightening into a tight ball. He hurried inside. "Get James, then, and we'll carry what we can to the second floor."

Water was now rushing into the storeroom, various items already beginning to float about. The three of them turned their attention to the flour barrel and hefted it onto a table. Meanwhile the distressed chicken was making the most ear splitting squawks Michael had ever heard. James went over and took it from a floating cardboard box where it had gone for protection. He put it on the window sill.

The water had now reached their knees and still rising. "Help me in the dining room," Michael shouted as he waded out of the storeroom and back to the kitchen. Matilda stopped to put the chicken in an empty pot on top of the stove. "Now you stay put," she said with a scorching look. "I ain't a gonna cook you. Yet."

Michael rushed through to the dining room. His heart sank when he saw water already swirling around the legs of the substantial mahogany table. The table and refurbished chairs were family heirlooms, a gift from his grandmother in Savannah for the grand opening of the hotel. "We can't move the table but we must get those chairs up off the floor," he said to James. They hefted the antique chairs, upholstered in a beautiful blue and gold tapestry, onto the table while Matilda began moving the sterling silver tea set and other valuables to the fireplace mantle. When the chairs were all elevated, he grabbed the new table linens from the sideboard drawers, ran up the stairs and dumped them on the bed, then started down for another armload. There would be time to sort everything later.

He was still on the stairs when he heard the shattering sound of glass breaking and the dining room windows burst in with an explosion of wind and water. Glass flew everywhere, the sideboard went over, the table with its load of chairs slammed against the wall with an unbelievable grinding and clatter.

"We all gonna be drown'd," Matilda screamed as she thrust a crystal vase high above her head. Michael navigated to her and grabbed her arm. The swirling water was gaining strength. He handed Matilda back to James, who was right behind him, and James slung her over his solid shoulder. Together they fought their way to the circular stairway and began to climb to the second floor bedrooms. But it seemed the water was rising faster than they could climb. The hurricane was slamming the house with its full force, the waves striking the building like a battering ram, the veranda going up and down like a bucking horse. Michael yelled, "This isn't safe. Head for the attic."

They scrambled up the narrow steps with Michael in the lead. Matilda grabbed his shirt. "I ain't goin' into that dark place," she cried in a quavering voice. "Theys haints up there."

Michael yanked himself free. "It's our only choice. The water is already on the second floor." He raced up the remaining steps and pushed open a trapdoor covered with spider webs. The attic was cramped, dark and un-floored, and Michael climbed over the rafters to a tiny window set in the western eave. By now the yard was part of the ocean, great waves chasing each other across from east to west, striking the trees with flying spray. As he watched, the chicken house lifted from its foundation and splintered into a thousand pieces. Parts of neighboring houses on Demere Road whizzed by, drawn by the demon wind. Great cedar trees, old as the nation, leaned into the wind and lay down. What his eyes saw his mind could not process and his heart refused to accept.

The boat he had secured so well went bobbing across the yard, still attached to the tree. He didn't know whether the tree was carrying the boat or the boat the tree. It seemed to be nip and tuck with them.

"Pray . . . pray," Matilda groaned from the attic stairway, firmly refusing to budge as the house trembled and shook.

In an instant there was a horrendous screaming noise as the roof buckled and let go, separating from the main body of the hotel and disappearing. Michael was blown through the opening and hurled into icy water. Desperately, he tried to swim but it was impossible in such churning foam. A piece of the roof banged against him and he grabbed it and hung on, working his arm through the V of a rafter still attached to the slate tiles. With a mighty effort he hoisted himself onto the temporary raft and struggled to keep the roof balanced. Rain, broken shells, and splintered driftwood lashed his face. The debris churning in the water was as menacing as the sea.

He was not alone. Rooftop rafts floated by, carrying children, dogs, and all manner of humanity. In seconds the force of the wind and water had transported him toward all that remained of a fishing dock, the splintered pilings like broken arrows ready to impale him. If he survived the waves, Michael was afraid he'd be dashed to pieces against the wreckage. Abruptly the wind veered and his raft was slammed against one of the huge live oaks still standing. He reached out and grabbed a branch, hanging on with every ounce of his remaining strength. It seemed like forever but it was only seconds before a wave threw him off the tree into a mass of drift where he lay, more dead that alive. Saltwater stung his eyes and clogged his throat. He vomited into the debris.

He lay there in the dreadful tempest of wind and rain, shaking and praying as he had never prayed before. He tried to yell for help but he seemed to have no voice left. His tears streamed down his cheeks as he realized the enormity of what had happened. *Were James and Matilda still alive? Had Amanda and his family safely reached Savannah? Was anything left of the resort and his two years of labor?* He lay half-buried in mud, fishing tackle, clamming rakes, barn doors, bits of carriages, dead birds, dogs, and cats for what seemed like hours. When the eye passed, and the storm delivered its final blow, people began moving about. A young boy saw him and went for help.

Several men dug him out and though considerably shaken none of his bones were broken. The water fell rapidly as the tide turned and the wicked wind moderated into a gentle breeze. he sought shelter and it was dusk before he could hobble across the island and up the beach toward what might be left of his hotel. The agonizing walk showed the damage to the sea shore, all the pretty cottages, bath houses, and docks were piled in one inextricable heap next to the woods. Houses sat in every imaginable condition, their yards full of broken furniture, carriages and animals. Some had the entire front wiped away, roofs were gone, or nothing was left standing but the chimney.

He staggered along, stone-cold, clothes muddied, bedraggled hair stuck with sand, face blackened with grime, legs bruised and bleeding.

It seemed as though nothing had been too heavy or strong to withstand the action of the waves. Michael's eyes stared with fascinated horror as several men tried to rescue two dolphins that had been washed ashore. A large ship had been left high and dry on Beachview Drive and the masts of other sailboats tilted at sickening forty-five degree angles. As he neared home he broke into a run, gulping air furiously, desperate, yet afraid, to see the end of his driveway. The roadway was choked with downed trees and he had to climb over a mass of drift before spotting the hotel. Built of tabby—a concrete-like mixture of lime, sand, and seashells—it was still standing though mangled and roofless, its porches gone. Hundred-year-old oaks were flat, their limbs crossed and tangled in every direction, while mingled with them were the remnants of chairs, tables, linens and crockery.

Thankfully, James and Matilda were alive. He could see them already busy trying to salvage what they could. Heart leaping, he limped to their side.

"Praise the Lawd, it's Master Michael," Matilda cried, wiping her face with her torn, muddy apron.

Reeling with unfettered joy he swept her into his arms. "God, I'm glad to see you alive. How did you make it?"

James smiled broadly. "When da roof sailed away with you on it, we tied ourselves together with ma rope belt an' climbed through the bedroom window. We grabbed on to a floating tree that came to rest halfway up Demere Road an' jest sat in dat ole tree till the storm over."

Michael looked around. It was hard to assimilate the damage wrought by the hurricane. Every outbuilding was either washed from its foundation, or blown away. The yard was a scene of complete devastation and ruin, debris several feet deep in places. The hotel was roofless and flooded. The parlor furniture, in-cludeing the fine new piano, was strewn over the beach. They found the boat, hard and fast, in the limbs of a tree on the edge of the myrtle hammock. Dead animals, both wild and domestic, lay everywhere. Michael's stallion, Hobie, and the two carriage horses were gone. A chicken, stripped of its feathers, limped across the lawn. Gulls and pelicans by the score had sheltered themselves about the hotel and after the storm waddled feebly into the ocean, unable to fly. Life or death seemed as random as the flip of a coin.

"Have we any livestock left?" Michael asked.

"Coupla our pigs was floundering in mud up to their bellies," Matilda answered. "James got 'em free. I been catching what chickens we got left and givin' 'em a good dunking in dat tub o' water."

"Well, come with me," Michael said to James. "I just passed several men trying to turn some endangered dolphins back into the water. I didn't stop because I was anxious to find you and Matilda and assess the damage to the hotel. Maybe we can help them."

"But you hurt, Masta Michael. You need cleanin' up," Matilda cried, shaking her head.

"I can wait. The dolphins can't." With that he turned and began to hurry down the beach, James behind him. The dolphins had been returned to the water but he saw men digging in piles of debris looking for people who might be trapped. Michael and James joined them, working by lantern light until Michael was too exhausted to stand. He draped his arm across James' shoulder and staggered back to the hotel.

Matilda had placed straw pallets on the floor of the butler's pantry—surprisingly intact after the storm—and Michael collapsed into the nearest one where he fell into exhausted sleep, muddy clothes and all.

The next day the sun was warm, the sky clear, the blue water sparkled back in its bed. But on land, desolation was everywhere. Michael started James and Matilda clearing away the rubble around the hotel while he set off for the mill to see if he could purchase some tar paper to give temporary protection where the roof was missing. As he drove his wagon down Demere Road, he was appalled to see that there was absolutely nothing left of John Gould's house except the chimney.

Several men he recognized from town were poking through the debris as though looking for something. "Where are the Goulds?" he asked.

"Out with a search party. Their children, little Jimmy and the baby, are missing. Mary was in the nursery with them when the wind blew out the window and sent the trunk of a cedar tree flying through the opening. It knocked her unconscious and the house just exploded from the wind. We can't find the little ones."

"Where are they looking?"

"In the marsh, yonder, while the tide is out."

Although still overwhelmed by his own disaster Michael realized the loss of family members would be far worse. He had been so wrapped up in the damage to his beloved hotel he had not given enough thought to the human carnage occasioned by the storm. He felt sick to his stomach. God demanded more of him.

In the distance he could see searchers spread out across the marsh and he immediately set out at a run to join them. He spied Mr. Gould wading through a narrow channel poking the shallow water with a long pole.

"Has anyone searched the beach?" Michael yelled.

"Not yet. The hurricane was moving this way."

"I'll go down along the dune line and look. Children are light and the wind fickle. The outgoing tide could have carried them toward the sea."

Michael retraced his steps to the beach and soon spotted several other search parties combing through the rubble lining the shore. He joined one group of men who informed him that three people were missing from the village as well as numerous pets. Feverishly they dug through stranded seaweed, tangled palm fronds and sodden Spanish moss. All of a sudden a shout rang out and everyone paused.

"The Gould children have been found," cried a man running along the beach.

"Are they all right?" several people shouted.

The man skidded to a stop. "Both dead," he said.

A sob caught in Michael's throat and he sank to his knees, his fists convulsing with suppressed rage. *Where was justice in all of this? Where was God?* A friend of his from the village approached him and placed a hand on his shoulder. "Rough it is," he murmured. He handed Michael a length of iron. "But we must keep digging in those downed trees. We've still got people missing."

They continued to work feverishly and silently. The dead body of a woman was recovered but she had thrown herself over her baby and miraculously the child was still alive. It was verging on dusk and lanterns were lit, but still they searched. At last, dog-tired and dejected he returned to the hotel where James was constructing a temporary coup for the surviving chickens.

"Let that be and go find Mr. Gould," Michael said. "Tell him he and his wife are free to live here till they can rebuild. They will want to be handy to their land."

"Did the mill have any tar paper left?"

"Truth be, James. I never got there."

"Probably all gone now."

"There is always tomorrow. God was good to us . . . all we lost were material things. Many people lost their lives."

"Still, I gonna add a little prayer tonight that He send no mo' rain till we get things covered up a bit."

Michael gave him a bittersweet smile. "You do that. And you might add a little footnote that the banking gods will see fit to direct some money our way to begin rebuilding."

As James walked away, Michael lowered himself onto the limb of a fallen tree and flexed his aching shoulders to ease the rigors of the long day. He sat absolutely still, listening intently to the noises of the night, the pounding of the surf, the small scuffing of nocturnal creatures, the slap of a lanyard against a wooden mast in gusting wind. An occasional shout could be heard from men still searching the beach. He held his head in his hands and squinted into the distant star-studded sky.

Had he the will to start over?

Chapter Two

October 1882
Chambersburg, Pennsylvania

The time had come. Somehow Abby had known it would come, but it didn't make it any easier. It was October—two months since the devastating hurricane blew ashore in Georgia, destroying her stepson's dream and making this action necessary.

She walked across the kitchen, opened the door and willed herself to listen to the echo of a sledge against a stake as Ford hammered the large "For Sale" sign into the ground. She leaned against the doorframe, her heart swelled with defeat and impotence at the sound of yet another blow driving the stake deeper into the rich Pennsylvania loam.

She covered her face with trembling hands. *Please, please dear God. Is there no other way?* she prayed.

This farm had been their home since the war ended and Ford returned from the South with his young son to claim her as his bride. They had weathered good and bad years as diphtheria took the life of their daughter, Molly, and Michael grew to maturity. The farm had flourished. Ford built a fish hatchery in the crystal, cold water of Falling Spring Creek and raised native brown trout which he shipped to the Pittsburgh and Philadelphia markets.

Now Michael had asked for their help to rebuild Ford's home in Georgia. He refused to give up after the hurricane but he had to start all over again. The rebuilding had been plagued with financial difficulties from the start. Ford had co-signed the original construction loan with a bank in Georgia but had no collateral for a second loan. He had tried to borrow money on the hatchery from the Chambersburg Trust with no success. The country had just emerged from the Panic of 1873 and money was still tight, but Abby had to admit that local banks had never been receptive to her husband. After all, he was a Southerner and the South had burned their town. Memories and resentments ran deep.

Ford came stomping into the kitchen. "That's done," he snapped. "Wonder how fast the news will spread. By tomorrow everyone in town will be whispering that the McKenzies are in trouble."

"We will simply tell anyone who asks that we are going to move south . . . back to your old plantation, to help our son."

"Don't kid yourself. Folks here have been just waiting to see me fail. You'll notice the locals still refer to this as the *Lehman Farm*." He gave Abby a keep-your-mouth-shut stare.

Ford was seldom short with her. She remembered the first time she saw him—a Confederate officer leaning against the wall of the Falling Spring Inn, whipcord-lean with dark copper hair brushed back from a face of distinct, hard angles. When he winked, her heart did a flip-flop like a fish caught in a net. Ford's hair was shot with gray now and he wore glasses but that wink, even after twenty years, still had the power to make her heart pound. She knew he was angry now, not at her, but because he heard an echo from the past. He had a lot of past and the echo was from the worst part.

Her brows furrowed deeply. "But things have been going well recently, dear. You are an officer in the Grange and just this year became a deacon at church." She gave him a mischievous grin. "People have forgiven you for being on the wrong side during the war."

"Hmm!"

"Things will work out, you'll see. I'm praying that God will help us make the right decisions." She took his hand and reached up to give him a kiss on the cheek. What she didn't say was that she was also praying that the farm wouldn't sell. She didn't want to live in the South.

•   •   •

Shortly after Thanksgiving Amanda put aside Michael's latest letter with a heart wrung with pity. He was determined to rebuild and had taken a job in order to secure lumber to replace the hotel roof. She lay wide awake in her college dorm after hours of waking, fitful dreams, dozing, then waking again. Tears stole down her cheek. She seldom wept. Why now? Guilt because her beloved was all alone with a monumental task while she pursued her own dreams?

Sleep was impossible so she slipped out of bed, pulled a dressing gown over her long nightdress and tiptoed past her sleeping college roommate. She took a wooden match from a matchbox, struck it, and lifted it to a gas lamp high on a wall bracket by her study table, turned the brass handle until she heard the soft hiss of gas, then applied the flame and settled in her rocker. She picked up the *Pharetra*, the school newspaper. Slowly, she raised it to catch the yellow pool of light from the lamp and began to reread the article entitled *Political Excitement*.

Yesterday a young woman, Lavinia Dock, a pacifist and radical suffragist, had been the featured speaker at a rally held in the college auditorium. She was at Wilson to sponsor a Women Rights march in Chambersburg next spring and was asking for volunteers. But she also was a nurse at Bellevue Hospital in New York and talked at length about the desperate need to develop training hospitals for nurses and raise the standards of a profession considered unfit for well-bred girls. Therein lay another reason for Amanda's restlessness. The speech had left her unsettled and confused.

Wilson students, like most other female college students, had not yet become active suffragists, but the issue of a woman's right to vote had sparked a debate on campus. In reply to the article in the *Pharetra* one student proposed that "a woman's right is only to be the glory and good angel of her home," while a second student suggested that those women who found the right to vote distasteful, should "go to unenlightened heathen lands and take their places there with the women who are treated as men's slaves and not as men's equals."

Amanda's face grew pensive. In two years she would graduate from Wilson College with a major in Liberal Arts, but what could she do with her degree? She was well read in the English classics, accomplished in French, Latin, and Art History. She was a member of the Literary Society of Chi Tau Pi, could play the piano, had learned all of the social graces, and was quite good at needlepoint. She rolled her eyes. *Ah, yes. Needlepoint. But nothing had fit her for the real world where disaster, poverty and illness were more the norms than the life of comfort she was expecting.*

She jumped to her feet, lips pursed, and threw the paper aside. The study parlor was warm and comfortable, silent except for the tiny hiss of the gas jets in their wall brackets. Amanda turned the key of the little green-shaded student lamp on her desk to extinguish the flame and stretched to ease the ache in her back. She noticed the exceptional light in the room and walked over to one of the high rectangle windows that looked down from her second floor room to the front lawn. She opened the drapes. It had begun to snow, unusual this early in the year. Big silver flakes were already piled several inches thick on the window sill. Though tired she did not feel like going back to bed. She'd been indoors too long and longed to get out into that glorious snow. A walk would relax her. It was just what she needed and with a smile she closed the drapes and walked to the closet, pulled overshoes over her high-buttoned shoes, selected her waterproof cloak, and wrapped a warm scarf around her head. The hall was empty of students at this hour, and she crept down the stairs to the first floor. Amanda glanced around but didn't see a soul. Good. Students were not allowed out of the buildings after eight o'clock but the stewards probably thought no one would want to venture out into a snowstorm. Rightfully so, she thought with a wicked grin.

Amanda walked out on the portico fronting the Main Building, the air sharp and still. Snowflakes settled on her woolen scarf and caught in her lashes, momentarily blurring the street lamps on Philadelphia Avenue already misty in the swirls of snow. The path that led to the street was completely obliterated. With a grin she furtively hiked her skirt up, tucked her chin into her collar and stepped into the powdery fluff, feet lifting high, overshoes clogged with wet snow. She tilted her head back, stuck her tongue out to catch the falling flakes and closed her eyes to enjoy the feel of this luminous night and her aloneness in it.

How lucky I am to be here, she thought, traipsing across the campus in the unexpected little winter snowfall. Wilson was a small woman's college with gracious native gray-stone buildings that looked more like Victorian homes than the barracks-like housing on many campuses. It was founded just after the Civil War expressly to serve the southern diocese of the Presbyterian Church in the education of young women. The college buildings curled along the banks of a lazy little stream called the Conococheague then later joined Falling Spring Creek and drained into the Chesapeake Bay.

The solitude was broken when beyond the silhouetted branches of the bare campus trees she heard a distant rhythmical jingle. As she listened, the tinkle of bells came closer. Down the center of the road she saw a sleigh drawn by a single horse trotting easily down the drifting street. The conveyance was open and snow-swirled cones of light under the street lamps revealed two people—a man and a woman. They sat, bundled snugly under a robe. She heard the woman laugh, her voice muffled, the sound distant and happy. Amanda felt a tug at her heart. She wished that she was with Michael under that warm robe, holding hands, laughing together. But, despite a set back in their plans, he was planning a life in the South—there would be no sleigh rides in the snow in Georgia.

The snow was getting deeper—too deep to walk with long skirts. Amanda turned back, but not before reaching down to gather a hand full of the white fluff to mold into a snowball. With a mischievous grin she hurled it after the departing sleigh.

The lobby was still deserted and she climbed the stairs without incident. Blue-edged flames flickered from gas jets on the wall of the long, deserted hall as she tiptoed her way past the locked doors of the other students. Stealthily, she turned her key in the big ornamented brass knob and opened her door.

She walked across the darkened room to a window facing the east campus, pulled up the heavy green window shade and opened the velvet drapes to stare out at the bright, silent moonlight. Trees were etched in charcoal against a lightening sky. The shadowy figure of a college guard carrying a lantern picked his way across the snow-covered lawn. Amanda slumped, drained of energy. Maybe she should try to get another hour of sleep. But after removing her dressing gown and heading back to bed she hesitated beside Esther Carbaugh's cot where her roommate was snoring softly. She was a little in awe of Esther. Her hair was naturally curly, not straight like Amanda's. Her grades were all straight A's, and she sang soprano solos in the Wilson choir. Amanda couldn't carry a tune for the life of her. Esther had a shell collection from summers at her beach home, and three manufactured ball gowns. Amanda had one gown and it was homemade. Esther had a father and a sibling—a big brother. Amanda was illegitimate with two half-sisters and a four-year-old adopted brother. Amanda stuck her chin out. At least she was a few months older, nineteen in fact, and almost engaged. Michael had announced his intentions but had not yet offered her a ring.

She sighed. That was an area she did not wish to visit just now.

Just before Wilson's Christmas break Amanda opened another letter from Michael, stroking its pages, savoring the anticipation of its content. Her eyes glinting with pleasure, she began to read:

My dearest Amanda,

I have a surprise for you. I have arranged to come north to see you and escort you to the Christmas dance.

I will be in Chambersburg for only two days because I can't afford to leave my job for much longer than that but I long to see you and hold you in my arms, even for just a few hours.

Put my name on every line of your dance card. I will share you with no one.

I should arrive by coach on Tuesday, next.

Till then, my sweetest,

Michael

Amanda bolted out of her chair, waving the letter at Esther who was lying on the bed reading a book. "He's coming! He's coming," she yelled.

Esther's eyebrows shot up in surprise. "Who's coming?"

"Michael. My Michael is coming from St. Simons for the dance."

"Maybe he will talk you out of entering the political arena and marching in that silly suffrage parade of Lavinia Dock's you've been chattering about for the past two days," Esther said hopefully.

"No, my mind is made up."

"Oh."

•   •   •

As the train rumbled through South Carolina Michael carefully opened the packet of lunch, wrapped in butchers' paper and tied with string, that his housekeeper had prepared for him. He smiled with pleasure. It was his favorite—wild duck on thick slabs of homemade bread and a block of goats' cheese. Matilda was an excellent cook and he planned to keep her on at the hotel when it opened. He drummed his fingers on the arm rest. *If it ever did.*

Michael ate everything down to the last crumb, washing it down with sweet iced tea from his canteen to which lemon had been added to mask the heavy sulfur taste of Georgia water. He leaned back against the seat and closed his eyes. How the years had sped by since he left Chambersburg for Charleston to find Greyhorse, his Native American father. He had been beset by anger then, anger at what he considered to be a lie when he found that Ford had failed to tell him of his true heritage. Since then he and Ford had resolved their differences and Michael was eager to see him. But Greyhorse had rejected him and Michael longed for the day he could flaunt his success in his father's face.

He allowed his thoughts to drift to Amanda. His beloved Amanda. She had just been entering college when he left, and she was in her Junior year now. As children he and Amanda had been playmates. They were cousins though not related by blood. Michael was seventeen when he first realized he loved her; nineteen, when he first spoke of that love to her. A future was spoken of but not planned. Too many unresolved issues stood in the way. Now, after the hurricane, there were new issues. He knew it would take years to rebuild, to get himself established to the point where he could support a family, but he had to try. He trusted that Amanda would wait for him.

The train was hotter than Hades and he pulled open his collar and sank deeper into his seat as the hypnotic clank of metal wheels on steel track lured him to sleep.

Tuesday evening, in his old bedroom on the Falling Spring Road, Michael pulled off his soiled travel clothes, walked to the dresser, poured water from the pitcher into its bowl, washed and shaved. He buttoned on a clean collar, donned black pants, tied his string-tie, combed his hair and quickly walked to the door. Tense with anticipation, he bounded down the stairs.

Tonight he would hold Amanda in his arms. Although all the girls would be heavily chaperoned, perhaps they could steal away for a few quiet minutes. Though brief, those stolen minutes were always intense. Together they would exchange confidences, he would tell her of the progress he was making in the South and the reason he must return so soon. What was the future for the two of them? He didn't know. All he knew was that tonight he would see her. He was content merely to be young, happy and in love.

•   •   •

That evening Amanda and Esther met in the study parlor to give each other final touches to their gowns and hair.

Esther's dress was of pale blue cashmere with trimmings of pearl beaded tulle, and a Marie Antoinette ruff with pearls. She wore a corsage of yellow roses. Amanda wore a gown of shimmering white China silk, the waist cinched, her plump arms covered with a stole of white lace and moire. She twirled around before a tall mirror and examined herself with critical eyes. She feared maturity would bring a weight problem—that she would tend to be heavy like her mother. Michael kidded her, saying that he liked some meat on his women, but she vowed to watch her diet.

She picked up a box of beautiful pink roses which had just arrived.

"Oh, how perfect," Esther said. Aren't you glad you talked your mother out of red velvet for your gown? These go perfectly with the white silk."

"Michael must have known I would wear white. Sometimes it seems we are so perfectly attuned to each other we can read each other's minds—even though we are separated by hundreds of miles," Amanda admitted.

"You are so lucky, dear. I must go to the ball on the arms of my brother."

A wall clock chimed. "Lawsy, we must go," Esther cried. "I'm on the receiving line. Miss Harmond will have my hide if I'm late."

Amanda descended the staircase into the lobby of Norland Hall carrying the bouquet of pink roses. She was met at the foot of the stairs by a young usher who hurriedly said, "Mr. McKenzie is in the music parlor waiting for you."

She rushed to meet him, her face flushed with happiness. Michael was standing just inside the door. His eyes were warm and welcoming as he stepped forward and gave her a kiss on the cheek.

Amanda fought to hide a grin. A shaving nick still bled on his right earlobe. Another cut was evident on his jawbone. He smelled of soap and antiseptic.

The refreshment room was aglow with light and beauty, decorated in the school colors of blue and silver. Colorful flowers adorned every table. All the folding doors had been rolled back and the Chambersburg Band was on hand to provide music.

The evening passed in a flurry of dancing, laughing, eating, and flirting. Amanda found herself thinking of nothing but sneaking away to be alone with Michael. Her reaction to the closeness of his body when they danced surprised and frightened her. The warm feeling that swept over her seemed very un-ladylike. A waltz was playing as Michael led her once around the dance floor then through an open French door onto a darkened corner of the veranda. He pulled her into his arms. "You are a little vixen," he said, "you have been batting those eyelashes at me all evening, fairly driving me crazy. Now make good on those promises your eyes have been making and give me a kiss."

His lips were soft, the kiss as gentle as any she could ever remember. She almost wished he were a little more aggressive. But that was Michael—always the perfect gentleman.

"It's a clear, crisp evening, let's take a walk," he suggested. "There's a lot we need to talk about."

They walked and walked. Down Philadelphia Avenue to Market Street, past the Rose Theater, the Court House, the Valley Bank, and P. Nicholas Furniture Company where Michael had worked and learned the carpentry trade.

As they walked, he talked. He was determined to rebuild but wanted to do more than simply replace the damaged structure. He wanted to add to the number of rooms and amenities but could not get the financing he needed. Meanwhile he was working at the lumber mill and putting every cent he earned into the hotel. So far he had only managed to replace the roof, but that enabled him to live at home. Then he spoke about things and feelings he had never shared with her. He talked about his stepmother, Abby, and what he had perceived as her rejection of him; about his half-sister Molly, the way diphtheria had claimed her life and changed his. Amanda listened carefully. She had heard most of the stories from her Aunt Abby but it seemed important that she hear them from him. He talked of his biological father. She sensed a bittersweet sense of pride in what he had learned of his Indian heritage.

And then she talked and he listened. She told him of her intent to help organize a suffrage march in Chambersburg in the spring. She had taken a science class this past year and was intrigued with the advances in medicine. She thought about going to graduate school but she had no clear-cut objective. She talked about her mother, Sarah, struggling to make ends meet after her stepfather's death. It was only through the largess of her uncle, Tom Kennedy, that Sarah was able to maintain their home at Coldbrook Farm and keep Amanda in college. Graduate school was probably out of the question.

A few drops of cold rain began to fall and they walked faster. They arrived back on campus to find it deserted and sought out a dark corner on the veranda. Raindrops began to ping on the tin roof and they moved further into the corner. He laid his palm against her cheek. "I know I promised to wait but I want you to come to St. Simons soon. I've been thinking about you a lot . . . day and night, in fact. And I've reached a decision. I think we should get married next spring."

Her heart began to pound. *Not this soon,* her mind screamed. *Not yet.*

"You said we would wait," she whispered. You said. . . ."

"I know. I know. It's just that it's harder than I thought. I want you with me. I need you."

Amanda bit her lip. There it was again. Michael wanted a helpmate—she wanted an education and purpose in life.

"Amanda . . . ?"

"I want to graduate."

He drew a deep breath. "You're right. I promised you could finish your education. But I want you to marry me just as soon as you have that diploma."

In lieu of a reply she threw her arms around him and kissed him, pressing close, swaying slightly to feel her body against his. She felt no shame in wanting to make him desire her. He looked astonished and she was overwhelmed by emotion. He held her tightly and she felt his arousal. She drew away, gazing at him, appraising his reaction. His breath was as warm as the rainy air. He put his hands on her hips and pulled her to him once more and they kissed again. His kiss, no longer gentle, was a revelation of what passion might lie ahead.

They held each other for a long time, talking in whispers, but she made no commitment to go south with him. And then they parted. Tomorrow Michael would return to St. Simons. Alone.

Chapter Three

A week after the Christmas dance Esther came running into the college dining room with exciting news. Her grandmother had sent her two train tickets to New York as a gift. Esther was to bring either a member of her family or a friend and could visit as long as she liked. Esther wanted Amanda to go with her.

Amanda was thrilled. She had never been to the big city and this was the perfect time. It would be all dressed up for the holidays.

Two weeks later on a frigid December morning during the holiday break Esther boarded the train in Pittsburgh after spending two days with her parents. Amanda climbed aboard in Harrisburg. They greeted each other with hugs and kisses, then settled back and began to chatter excitedly.

"I have a surprise for you," Esther said. "My brother, George, is meeting us in New York. Mother refused to let me go to the *big city* without a chaperone."

"But I thought he had a job before going on to law school."

"He does. Have a job that is. And get this . . . get this . . . it's in New York and he's staying with my grandmother. He changed his major from law to medicine. Now he wants to go to Paris to study. Father is having a fit. It's a long story."

Amanda gave Esther a searching look. "George is nice and all, but remember I'm practically engaged to Michael. I hope you aren't planning to act as match maker."

The dimple in Esther's cheek deepened. "Oh, I wouldn't dream of it."

•   •   •

George met the two girls at Grand Central Station. Amanda gave him an apprising look. His eyes were friendly and bright with intelligence. His hair was red-brown, thick and wavy, and he had grown a full drooping mustache since she had last seen him. He was dressed in what she supposed the gentlemanly men of Harvard wore—black pants, black buttoned shoes, wide suspenders over a green-and-white-striped shirt, and a black vest with a heavy gold watch chain draped across the front. Quite a dandy. He kissed them both on the cheek, grabbed their small valises—they had shipped their luggage ahead—and led them out onto the teeming sidewalk. Amanda gasped at the noise as they began walking the short block from the train to the elevated station: traffic rumbling and pounding on the cobblestone street, the ring of harness bells and clop-clop of hoofs on cobbles, drivers shouting and fighting for the right of way.

"Grandmother lives at the Dakota, way up in the boondocks, in what they call Upper New York," he said. "I thought we would take the El. It's an overhead train, and quite a unique way to see the city for the first time. We catch it at the Third Avenue station and ride it all the way from downtown to its last stop at Sixth Avenue and Fifty-Ninth Street."

They climbed the iron steps to the little station. The waiting room was windowless and gloomy, lit by a single tin-shaded kerosene ceiling lamp reflecting on worn floorboards and dark wooden tongue-and-groove walls. There were several cuspidors, ringed by errant tobacco juice, emitting a foul odor and a change-booth with a funny little protruding shelf scooped out for customers to collect their change and tickets. George shoved three nickels through the little half-moon hole in its grill and received three tickets.

Neither Amanda nor Esther had ever ridden on an El and they walked out to the platform, crowded with waiting passengers, with trepidation. Then a whistle toot-toot-tooted and they looked down the tracks to see a short, squat, locomotive huffing toward them, red sparks and white steam flaring into the air from its stack.

There were three cars, enameled light green and trimmed with gilt arabesques. Inside, upholstered benches ran the length of the car which was nearly filled. George led them to a seat near the front. They had hardly sat down before a bearded, conductor in a blue uniform came through the car collecting tickets. After starting up, the train immediately took a sharp curve to the left and George explained they were crossing busy Forty-Second Street. As the El rumbled through the city it stopped for only seconds at each station. Amanda would have been terrified of missing their stop had George not been with them. They got off at the end of the line and made their way down to street level, then walked through a village green called Central Park. A large building loomed in the distance.

George slowed as they approached the Dakota to let them take in its splendor.

"Holy Smoke," Amanda gasped. "She lives here?"

"That she does. It's a new residential hotel . . . and huge. Some of the apartments have seventeen rooms." He grinned. "O'ma, my grandmother, doesn't have quite that many but she does have a living room, dining room, library, kitchen and three bedrooms."

The Dakota was eight stories of brick and stone and covered an entire block. Rounded columns of bay windows opening onto balconies of carved stone rose vertically on both sides of the building into roof top cupolas.

A uniformed doorman greeted George and waved them through the lobby and a large arch that opened into a roofless area. The Dakota was built around a courtyard with several spectacular big bronze fountains that must be beautiful in the summer. A huge Christmas tree decorated with hundreds of white candles, white angels and silver bows graced the open space. George led them to a wide staircase in the northeast corner and, huffing and puffing, they climbed to O'ma's apartment on the sixth floor. Groaning from the exertion George slipped a large key into an ornate brass keyhole and opened the door.

Esther's grandmother came sweeping into the entry. She was a tall, regal woman with short-cut, steel-gray hair, a rather long nose, and wire glasses that framed dark eyes. She gave Esther a deep hug of affection, then folded Amanda's small hand into her own cool, dry palm. "I'm so happy to meet you, Miss Kennedy. Esther has written fondly of you."

"As she has talked of you, Mrs. Bruner. It is most generous of you to invite me to your home."

"Please, dear . . . call me O'ma as my grandchildren do. It's German for Grandmother. Now come into the parlor and bring me up to date on your activities."

A maid appeared with a silver tray of tea and scones. She was young and wore a gray dress with a long green apron and a jaunty little white cap. Amanda noticed a flush on her cheeks when she passed the tray to George.

"You can take the girl's valises to their quarters, Mary," O'ma said as she settled herself in a high-backed wing chair. She smiled apologetically. "I'm afraid you girls will have to share a room. This apartment only has three bedrooms and George has been an unexpected, but most welcome, guest."

With a nod George said, "And if you will excuse me I'll retire to that room and leave you girls to talk. I have some reading to do."

While Esther filled her grandmother in on events at college and at home Amanda looked around the elegant room with interest. The large living room was decked out for Christmas with a roaring fire and a towering tree. It was papered in a muted silver and green stripe with a large ornate mirror trimmed in gold gracing one wall. The ceiling was beamed and the tall, rectangular windows were hung with heavy green damask and strung with an evergreen garland. French doors opened onto what Amanda guessed was one of the balconies she had seen from below.

O'ma walked over to a pull-cord by the mantle and summoned the maid. "You girls would probably like to freshen up before dinner," she said.

They walked behind the maid along the long carpeted hall. Amanda glanced into the rooms they were passing: a formal dining room, a library lined with books, a fully equipped kitchen, and two closed doors of what she guessed were bed-chambers.

The maid opened the last door and showed them in. A heavy carved bedstead dominated the room. Across from the bed was a dark wood dresser with porcelain knobs and a marble top. A small table, covered with a gold, tassel-fringed cloth sat between two tall windows that looked down onto a lake and the woods of Central Park. A wooden rocker was in front of one of the windows while the other had a window seat covered in gold velvet. It was a large room, papered in a bold gold and green cabbage print. An oriental rug of warm colors covered the floor.

Esther flopped on the bed. "I don't know about you, but I'm dead tired. I hope dinner isn't too long and drawn out. I'll tell O'ma we want to retire early. Tomorrow we get to see the *big city*."

Amanda was up before dawn and spent an hour dressing. O'ma had warned her to dress warmly so she put on a camisole, flannel pantaloons and cotton combinations, then a maroon wool dress with a round white collar and cuffs. Lastly, she pulled on her new street boots. Before leaving for New York she had spent what felt like hours standing with a pail of sand in each hand to make a firm impression on a length of leather while a bootmaker traced the outlines of her feet. The boots were soft leather and pliable. Although still new they felt wonderful.

Esther was already in the dining room eating breakfast and George was on his second cup of coffee when she arrived at the table.

"Hurry up slow poke," he teased. "Your carriage awaits you."

"Good morning to you, too," Amanda said.

After a quick breakfast she removed her ankle-length black coat from the armoire in the hall and wrapped a wool scarf around her head. She was ready for whatever the *big city* held.

Although there was a line of hacks in front of the hotel, George led them though the park to catch a little wooden, horse-drawn bus stopped along the curb on Fifty-Ninth Street. Amanda hopped onto the jutting wooden step at the rear of the bus, followed by Esther and George. The driver sat high on an out-side seat at the front of the conveyance and after a cursory glance in their direction he snapped the reins and they jolted forward.

Inside, two empty benches ran the length of the bus. They walked forward to the tin box labeled FARE – Five Cents. George dug three nickels from his pocket and dropped them in. Amanda giggled when she saw the driver glancing down through a hole in the roof to see that they had paid and mis-chievously she waved up to him.

She and Esther sat, heads swiveling, trying to see out both sides of the bus at once. They were driving through tree-lined streets of tall, dignified three and four story brownstones, many of them fronted by a neat patch of lawn. People strolled sedately—men in ankle-length great coats and tall shiny silk hats, younger men in shallow low-crowned derbies, women in long fur coats and elaborately feathered hats.

Amanda jumped at the sound of a gong. A dark-green enameled wagon was turning off Fifty-Fifth into Fifth Avenue.

She could see gold-leaf lettering printed along its side that said *St. Luke Hospital.*

The wagon turned into a driveway curving to the right just ahead of them and then stopped before a large gray stone building with very tall round-topped windows.

"That's where I work," George said with a smile.

"Hmm," his sister said. "You don't seem to be working very hard."

"I called in a favor with another chap when I knew you were coming. We traded days off." He glanced at Amanda from the corner of his eye. "I wanted to show you the sights. I must be back to work tomorrow, though."

Esther said, "I can't imagine you doing any kind of maintenance work. Our mother could never get you to do anything around the house."

"Well, I didn't have to, did I? With all the help we had. I never saw you do much either."

Amanda thought she had better interrupt what could turn into an argument. She looked at George. "Do you happen to know a nurse named Lavinia Dock?" she interjected.

George looked puzzled. "A nurse? No, I'm afraid not. We really don't talk to nurses. Why? Is she a friend of yours?"

"No, she is a young lady who gave a very inspirational lecture at college. She is training at Bellevue Hospital." Amanda frowned. She hadn't liked the scorn in his reply, but then neither had she defended Miss Dock's profession.

"Bellevue lies along the river on the Lower East Side . . . around First Street I believe," he said. "It's a pauper hospital. Our tour doesn't take us there."

Amanda watched from the window of the bus as the driver of the wagon jumped to the ground and tied the horse to a post. A man in an ankle-length white coat came out of the hospital, the tail gate on the wagon was lowered and the two of them slid a wooden and canvas stretcher out the back. As the bus passed the hospital, they saw a woman lying motionless on the stretcher being carried quickly up the stone steps and inside.

The bus rattled on over the cobbles and Amanda's thoughts drifted to Lavinia Dock and the speech she had given at Wilson. Lavinia had seemed so positive about the course her life was going to take—she was going to train at Bellevue and planned to help Lillian Wald establish a settlement house on the Lower East Side. Amanda knew nothing of the life of the immigrant poor. She was far from rich but life had always been good to her. She did not worry about the thousands that Lavinia talked about, starving and reeking with disease in city slums. She simply couldn't imagine it. *Still*, she wondered. *Just where is the Lower East Side? If there is time I would dearly love to visit it while I'm here.*

Esther, her face pressed to the glass of the bus as they rolled down Fifth Avenue, let out a whoop. "There it is. St. Patrick's Cathedral. Oh, Amanda, look . . . it is massive. It takes up an entire block."

The bus was passing directly before the imposing church now. The pale gray cathedral with its huge three-story bronze entrance completely filled the windowpane. Amanda's gaze swept the famous rose window and majestic three-hundred-foot stone towers at the front of the cathedral. She was awe-struck, full of wonder at the magnificent edifice.

Stops were more frequently now. A man climbed in, dropped his fare in the tin box, and sat down across the aisle from them with a casual disinterested glance. Judging from those she saw Amanda noticed that New Yorkers seldom made eye contact with strangers and never spoke to them.

The driver slapped his reins and the bus rolled on, the only sound the hard rattle of the iron-tired wheels on cobbles. Amanda pressed her hand against the frosted window to clear a spot from which she could watch as the cross streets slipped by—Forty-Ninth, Forty-Eighth, Forty-Seventh—row after row of silent brownstones. Then, as they moved to the thick of the city, the streets became more lively and small shops advertised their goods with elegant signs. They passed the Windsor Hotel, the Sherwood, and Henry Tyson's Fifth Avenue Market. A glittering parade of carriages was going in all directions, delivery wagons pulled by dray horses strained with effort, flat-bedded drays hauling barrels rumbled and pounded on the cobbles. Nearly every vehicle had four iron wheels that smashed and rang and every horse had ironclad hoofs. Wheels clattered, wood groaned, chains rattled, whips cracked, and men cursed and shouted. Amanda held her hands against her ears, transfixed by the pandemonium. Esther and George laughed at her. They were from Pittsburgh and more attuned to city traffic, but she was a country girl. This was like Chambersburg on Market Day only ten times more wild.

At the next intersection the bus edged to the curb and with sparkling eyes George led the girls to the exit. He was about to show them the city and he was clearly excited about it. On the corner of Broadway a mustached policeman in a tall helmet and white gloves was directing traffic with a slim baton and the graceful motions of a symphony conductor. Traffic flowed through the intersection, majestic prancing horses with heads high and manes braided pulled glittering carriages in brilliant colors of rich maroons, canary yellow and olive-green.

"You girls must see Ladies Mile," George said, taking Amanda's arm to cross the street. Esther watched him with a small smile.

"What is Ladies Mile?" Amanda asked.

"Block after block of ladies' stores stretching all the way to Eighth Avenue. Come on, I'll show you."

It was glorious. The sidewalks and entrances of the women's stores had display windows that reached to within a foot or so of the sidewalk. Most of the windows were protected by waist-high polished brass bars. Women, standing shoulder to shoulder in fashionable wool coats with fur hats or scarfs, their hands tucked into warm muffs, crowded the sidewalks admiring the displays. When a woman and her companion moved away Amanda slipped past her and Esther followed. The window was filled with gloves, some in fancy boxes, most on plaster display arms.

"Look at that purple pair," Esther said. "It has eighteen buttons."

Amanda nodded, her lips moving as she counted a black pair. "Twenty buttons," she whispered.

They moved to another window displaying hats, then another window and still another before George grew impatient and took each of them by the arm.

"Enough of ladies finery," he said. "I want to show you something in Madison Square."

They strolled along the thronged streets of Manhattan past jewelers, confectioners, drugstores, restaurants, cigar stores and hotels. Many offices, barbershops and restaurants were below the street level, something Amanda had never imagined. They went by Lord and Taylor—a store Amanda had often heard mentioned and at Nineteenth Street they stopped to gaze in the windows of a magnificent store of white marble bearing a bronze plaque that read "Arnold Constable & Company." Small boys shined shoes from portable stands carried around their neck. Men wearing brightly painted sandwich boards ambled along with elaborate advertisements. There were street venders: a man with a wooden sling around his neck filled with apples, another man with a basket of puppies for sale, a woman selling toys from a basket, and a one-armed man playing a lively tune on a grind organ with a monkey on his shoulder.

They walked up Eighth Street to Madison Square Park between Thirty-First and Thirty-Third Street. A German band was playing and after they stopped to listen to a sprightly tune George dropped several coins into a felt hat lying at their feet. Out of the blue Esther grabbed his arm.

"What in the world is that?" she asked gawking in disbelief as she stared at something on the edge of the park.

George chuckled. "That's what I brought you here to see." The erect right arm of the Statue of Liberty was standing on the west side of Madison Square holding the lighted torch of liberty high above the surrounding trees.

As they walked toward it, George explained. "The statue is a gift from France. But this is only the arm. The French designer, Bartholdi, completed both the head and torch-bearing arm before the statue was fully designed and it was shipped to Philadelphia for the centennial exposition. The entire statue is not yet complete. It will be erected in the harbor someday if New York-ers can ever decide where to put it. Right now the arm and torch are on display to raise money to construct the pedestal."

The clenched right hand was gigantic, fingernails as large as a sheet of writing paper with the great copper torch gripped in that hand as tall as a three-story building. High above them people looked down from an ornate railing surrounding the base of the flame.

"I want to go up," Amanda said.

"Anything my lady desires," George said as he took her elbow with a flourish.

Esther gave them an angelic smile.

Together they climbed a narrow circular stairway inside the arm, then stepped out onto the railed walkway. Amanda gazed across Madison Square. In the distance she could see the helmeted traffic cop, Ladies Mile with its crowd of elegant women, and men in tall silk hats thronging the busy street.

Amanda loved it. She could live in a city like this. She closed her eyes to stop the sting of unexpected tears from uncon-trollable joy.

The week passed in a blur. On Sunday Amanda, Esther and Mrs.

Bruner attended Mass at St. Patrick's, Monday they visited the Museum of Natural History, a few blocks north of the Dakota, and Tuesday George took them to the Rialto, the theatrical section of New York, to see Lillian Russell at Tony Pastor's new Fourteenth Street theater. It was obvious George was attracted to Amanda and she had to admit she was attracted to him. He always managed to sit between her and Esther, his shoulder seeming to accidentally touch hers. Wednesday was an especially full day as they made a trip on the El to Battery Park, took a ferry ride and strolled through the financial district. That evening they attended a lecture by Oscar Wilde at Chickering Park. Evenings were spent in O'ma's parlor singing old favorites: "I'll Take You Home Again," "Kathleen," "In the Evening by the Moonlight" and "Oh, Dem Golden Slippers," while O'ma played along on her small wooden organ. George had a beautiful baritone that blended with Esther's soprano. Amanda was usually off key but still joined the fun and sang along.

Thursday morning, as they finished a delicious breakfast, O'ma gave Amanda a smile. "What would you like to do today," she asked?

"I'd really like to see the Lower East Side and Bellevue Hospital."

All conversation stopped, the only sound in the room the silent hiss of the gaslights from the overhanging chandelier.

"Surely you don't mean that, Child. Mercy, the East Side is the tenement district . . . it's terribly unsafe. I couldn't possibly allow you to go there."

George was sitting with his fork halfway to his mouth. "Why, the East Side for heaven's sake?"

"You remember I asked you if you knew a nurse named Lavinia Dock? Lavinia's lecture at Wilson affected me very deeply. I was quite taken with her and . . . well, I haven't been able to get her off my mind. I would like to talk to her again if she is still there."

"Surely, you aren't thinking of becoming a nurse," O'ma said.

"No, but I am restless. I don't know why. I just feel that I want to do something worthwhile with my life, more than what I am being prepared for." She looked at the floor and worked the edge of the rug with the toe of her shoe. "You know . . . to meet new people with new ideas."

Esther looked at her knowingly. George just frowned.

"I'm filling in for a friend on the night shift tomorrow," he said. "If you really want to go, I could take you down there in the morning."

Amanda gave him a grateful smile. "Thank you, George. It does mean a lot to me."

So, she and Esther spent the rest of that day investigating Central Park, watching children sail little wooden boats in the lake and feed the ducks. That evening everyone retired early but the Dakota's new steam heat made the bedchamber stifling hot and Amanda could not fall asleep. At last she rose, put on a heavy dressing gown and knitted slippers, walked across the darkened living room and slipped out onto the concrete balcony. A chill wind ruffled her loosened hair and she gave a sigh of relief as she leaned against the railing.

Below her, on the street, a man moved before dimly lighted doorways carrying a long pole and as he walked he reached up into darkened street lamps and touched them to light. Across the way a full moon showed the ghostly curves and shadows that were the paths of Central Park. New York and its diversity of people were whole new worlds to her. She was standing quietly musing about Lavinia Dock's lecture concerning social consciousness when she looked up to see George framed in the doorway.

She gave a little gasp of surprise and he looked as startled as she.

"I was having trouble going to sleep," he stammered.

"Me, too. You're welcome to join me."

"I'll just lean against the rail for a few minutes to catch a breath of air. That is if you don't mind."

"Not at all." They fell quiet, not looking at each another. Amanda fought to hide a smile. He looked rather cute. His nightshirt was stuffed into his trousers, his hair badly tousled, and he was barefoot.

"You are a funny girl," he said with a hint of a smile. "Not at all like the other women I know. Most of them are only interested in making a good marriage and raising a family. I sense a yearning for much more in you."

"You, of all people, should understand. You are apparently going against your parent's wishes to embark on a career of your own choosing. I think it very admirable to dream of an adventure as challenging as going to Paris to study medicine."

George sighed. "So far it's just that . . . a dream. My dad is a lawyer and he expects me to take over his firm someday. He is a very controlling person. It would be much easier to do what he wants. But, Amanda, such exciting new discoveries are being made in medicine every day. This spring the German scientist Robert Koch discovered bacillus and last month he announced that he had isolated the germ that causes tuberculosis. Law seems dull and boring compared to that."

They fell silent again. After several minutes George pushed himself away from the rail. "Goodnight," he said. "I'll see you in the morning and we will embark on your little adventure."

"Goodnight."

The next morning Esther said she had no interest in seeing the tenements so she and O'ma set out to do some shopping. Meanwhile, George engaged a hack and he and Amanda started south to tour the Lower East Side.

"Do you have any particular place in mind?" George asked.

"Not really. Miss Dock, the lecturer I mentioned yesterday, expressed an interest in serving at a settlement house on the Lower East Side. It sounded like another world and I was curious."

"It is another world—largely inhabited by those newly arrived from the Deep South and the immigrants who were drawn there from the clearing room of Ellis Island." He tapped the driver on the shoulder. "Make a loop."

The driver turned the carriage east on a broken roadway named Hester Street. There was no asphalt, although Amanda had noticed that the brownish-black material was beginning to be established in other parts of the city. Through Hester and Division Streets they rode, passing the marketplace with its stinking fish stands and evil-smelling leavings. Throngs of people intensified the odor which assailed them from every side and Amanda discreetly raised a handkerchief to her nose. The driver turned again on Henry Street and they entered the great teeming streets of the East Side where most of New York's immigrant populations lived. Tall reeking houses jammed hard against the sidewalks, many with windows of cardboard or tattered sheets. It was a part of the city that Amanda felt most of America did not know existed. She certainly hadn't. If Americans knew, surely they would do something about it.

Streets by street—Grand, Broome, Spring, Prince, First, Second, Third—they rolled through the ethnic communities: Jewish, Italian, Irish, Chinese, Black. Amanda was wordless. Each looked like a foreign country. The poverty of some of these neighborhoods was beyond words, beyond her comprehension. The ethnic groups flowed into one another and she could only tell where one neighborhood began and another community ended by the appearance of its inhabitants: the yarmulkes of the Jews, the black skin of the Negro, the shops and dress of the Chinese. George pointed them out as they drove by and told a little about each. Amanda felt stupid and naive . . . and very young.

She was silent as the driver piloted the carriage down the littered streets. Suspicious eyes followed their carriage as it slid through their neighborhood and Amanda felt a sliver of fear. George warned her not to make eye contact with anyone and she didn't.

"Have you seen enough?" he asked. "Or do you want to see Bellevue Hospital."

"No," she whispered. "I've seen enough."

He smiled and looked relieved.

Part Two

1884-1888

Chapter Four

Two years had passed. The year was 1884; Grover Cleveland was the first bachelor president, there were thirty-eight states in the Union, and Mrs. Belva Lockwood, a prominent woman lawyer ran for president of the United States on an Equal Rights ticket. The men of Rahway, New Jersey tried to ridicule her by parading in dresses and striped stockings but everyone laughed at the men instead. And in June Amanda Kennedy graduated from Wilson College and joined Lavinia Dock in a suffrage march in Harrisburg, Pennsylvania campaigning for a woman's right to vote. They were splattered with eggs and tomatoes for not understanding "their place."

Chambersburg was bustling with new commerce. It had its bright days and dark ones, its seedtime and its harvest, the same as years before and like those yet to come. The local newspaper, *The Valley Spirit*, bragged that ninety-eight new buildings had been built last year; that it took only one hour to go from Chambersburg to the magnificent park at Mt. Alto on a new spur of the Cumberland Valley Railroad, and that plans were moving forward for the Centennial Anniversary of Franklin County in September. They bemoaned the outbreak of hog cholera on neighboring farms. Front Street had been renamed Main Street and residents shopped at the new Cressler's Drug Store that advertised Patent Medicines, Horse and Cattle Powder, combs, toilet soap, perfumery, hair oil, braces and trusses.

• • •

On a sultry Tuesday morning, shortly after graduation, Amanda left home to meet Abby for lunch at the Washington Hotel. She wore her new riding skirt with a modest split down the middle designed for horseback and bicycle riding, a white blouse high at the neck, and a pillbox hat. She had always looked to her aunt for advice, rather than her mother, and she needed it now. She was more convinced than ever that she wanted to do something worthwhile with her life. Just what, she still didn't know. Unfortunately, Amanda and her mother, Sarah, were like oil and water. They had never communicated well. Besides, Sarah hated anything Southern. She only tolerated Uncle Ford because he was married to her sister and donated money toward the upkeep of Coldbrook. Hoping to avoid questions from her mother, Amanda slipped out the back door, skirted the front of the house and hurried down the curving stone path bordered by great clumps of pink tulips and yellow daffodils. She crossed the little humpbacked stone bridge spanning the gurgling creek. It was a gorgeous day of blue skies with fleecy white clouds. Amanda halted on the minuscule bridge to watch for the flickering flash of trout darting under shadowy creek stones, then followed the farm lane out to Market Street. She moseyed down the street past the row of five connected town houses on the northwest corner of Fourth Street called by locals "Wanamaker Row." Nelson and Elizabeth Wanamaker were good friends to her mother. They had settled in Chambersburg from Philadelphia but their son remained behind to found what was becoming a world famous department store. Continuing west, she passed the grandiose mansion of Colonel Thomas B. Kennedy, president of the Cumberland Valley Railroad and her mother's boss. Ironically the Colonel's home had been built by Judge Riddle, the builder of her home. Humming softly and swinging her reticule, Amanda crossed the street at Third Avenue and entered the front door of the Washington Hotel, known for its excellent meals. Aunt Abby was waiting for her in the spacious lobby, smiling broadly, her face flushed with good cheer.

"My, but don't you look happy," Amanda said.

"Oh honey, and I am. I just received a letter from Michael. Have you heard from him lately?"

"No, not for several weeks."

"Let's go inside and order. I'll tell you all about it."

Amanda had never seen her aunt so radiant. After they were seated and had ordered the hotel's famous crab cakes, Abby reached into her reticule and drew out a letter. "Ford and I received this yesterday. It has the most wonderful news. Michael is returning this fall to finish college in Gettysburg."

"What?"

Abby beamed. "Can you believe it? He went to see his grand-mother in Savannah . . . it was just a social visit, mind you . . . and during dinner she said she would pay his tuition if he returned to Pennsylvania and finished his education. And . . . get this . . . if he graduated she would sell her house in Savannah and move back to St. Simons. She would finance the rebuilding of McKenzie Groves and have Michael build her a small cottage somewhere on the grounds." A shadow moved across Abby's face. "She wants to be buried on the island at Christ Church beside her husband."

Amanda could only blink in stunned surprise.

Abby thrust the letter at her. "You will probably get a letter today but read mine." Her gray eyes crinkled mirthfully. "The first thing I did was run down and yank that hated 'For Sale' sign out of our front lawn."

Amanda quickly scanned the letter then handed it back to her aunt. "I'll bet Uncle Ford was surprised. How does he feel about all this?"

Abby made a production of placing her napkin on her lap. "Maybe he is a little disappointed that we will not be returning to the island. Nevertheless, he is pleased. You know how much he wanted Michael to go to college. And, of course, this settles the financial problem." She gave Amanda a long searching look. "You don't seem as exuberant as I thought you would be. Michael is coming home. Aren't you excited?"

Amanda felt a hue of shame. Of course she was happy that he would be coming home, but mostly she felt relief. Michael had two more years of college, then he would be occupied for another year rebuilding the hurricane-damaged hotel. This would give her time. *Time for what?* She fidgeted in her seat.

Her aunt noticed and frowned. "Amanda, you seem different lately. You seem troubled."

"I know."

"Are you and Michael having problems? Tell me plainly, Amanda. Do you intend to marry him?"

Amanda's gaze shifted to her lap. "Who else would I marry? I have never dated another boy. I have cared for Michael since I was a child."

"I notice the absence of the word love. Honey, never play with a man's heart. I think that is one of the worst things our gender can be guilty of."

"Oh, I do love him, Aunt Abby. I didn't mean to infer that I didn't. And I know he loves me. It's just that he sees me as a wife and mother . . . nothing more. When I mention a career, he steers away from the subject as though it is something I will grow out of. I asked you to have lunch with me today because that is just what I wanted to talk about. I have been thinking of becoming a nurse or a social worker. It is something I could combine with marriage if Michael would allow me."

"But nursing is not a career for educated girls like yourself."

"That is changing, Aunt Abby. Women like Florence Nightingale, Clara Barton, Lillian Wald and Lavinia Dock are revolutionizing nursing and changing it into a respected profession."

"It would require several years of schooling, wouldn't it?"

"At least two. And I would have to go to Philadelphia or New York. But don't you see if Michael is going back to college that would work for me."

Just then the waiter brought their sandwiches and for the next few minutes they were busy with their lunch. Her aunt was silent, her face pensive. Eventually, in a quiet voice she spoke. "You say you love Michael. But, honey, it's not enough just to be in love. Marriage is about how you spend your days with each other, who you choose as friends, and most of all it's about how you build a life together. You say you want to be a nurse or social worker. If you give it up to spend your life being only a wife and helpmate you will end up resenting him. And even if he says he will give you permission to pursue your dream, he will expect you to be a partner in the hotel. He will come to resent you, too."

Amanda squared her shoulders and looked into her aunt's eyes. Instead of speaking she smiled, and not a very complacent or submissive smile either. "So," she said. "What do I do?"

"Have you heard about the formation of a Children's Aid Society in Chambersburg?"

"No, I haven't."

"The state of Pennsylvania recently passed legislation mandating that children between the ages of two and sixteen cannot be kept in poorhouses longer than sixty days. A number of our local residents met at the Central Presbyterian Church and voted to establish a home for the children in Franklin County. Mind you, these poor homeless and abused children are now kept in the county jail. Dr. Suesserott and several attorneys in town will remove these children and place them in the care of a Children's Aid Society. More than a score of children are awaiting the opening of a home. Unfortunately, there no funds for a house, clothing, or provisions to feed or help care for them. John G. Orr, one of the directors and an owner of *The Valley Spirit* has volunteered to use his newspaper in a drive to solicit donations."

"Oh, I know Mr. Orr. He is an elder in our church."

"That's right. He is. John Orr is quite an interesting man and very active in the General Assembly of the Presbyterian Church. His family founded the village of Orrstown just north of here and he worked as a banker in Carlisle before coming to Chambersburg to purchase *The Valley Spirit* with his brother. I think this is something that might interest you. It seems a very worthwhile endeavor."

Amanda nodded her head. "Now that you mention it, I did hear some women discussing it at a recent Grange meeting. Blanche Coyle and Maggie Sweeney said they were directors of the new Children's Aid Society. I'll look into it, Aunt Abby. If I could secure a job there, I might be able to use that experience on the island. I could establish an orphanage at St. Simons if they don't already have one."

Abby took a sip of her tea. "The idea that you are thinking of a career takes me by surprise. I'm not sure how to advise you. When Ford and I married, I found that, like most Southern men, he tended to put me on a pedestal. He was not willing to let me help with the business affairs of the hatchery until just recently." She grinned. "He had a fit when I told him I wanted to march with the suffragettes."

"I remember."

"Have you talked to your mother about this?"

"Not really. John is still a child; he keeps her busy. In addition she is working full time and still struggling to learn how to use the typewriter. And, as you know, she is keeping time with Peter Wingert."

"Yes, I know and he seems like a fine gentleman. Let me think about this. I certainly wouldn't advise you to marry if you had any doubts. Marriage has enough pitfalls without entering into it with uncertainty. I've found that life has many peaks and valleys. It is sad and difficult. We often hurt those we love most. Oh, my dear, it's a glorious thing to love, but it can bring you great pain, too." She picked up half of her sandwich. "Now let us enjoy these delicious crab cakes and leave weighty subjects for another day."

Before going home Amanda scurried up to J. N. Snider's Booksellers on the Square to get a copy of *Anne* a popular novel by Constance Fennimore Woolson about the life of a young orphan. Her mother had asked her to pick up some tea so she crossed the street to Lortz and Wolfganger Grocery and bought it along with some peppermint sticks for Eliza, Erin and John. Her final stop was in the new brick building housing both the Post Office and the Chambersburg Deposit on the southeast corner of the square. The letter she hoped for, a long tan envelope like the ones Michael always used, was there. She eagerly snatched it up and hurried home.

Coldbrook Farm stood on the crest of a wooded knoll, surrounded by landscaped grounds in the center of the beautiful, mountain-girded Cumberland Valley. Dating from early in the century, Coldbrook was considered a gentleman's farm, containing a large stone house, a frame fore-bay bank barn, a wagon shed and a stone, gable-roofed spring house. Two streams of cold, clear water flowed into Falling Spring Creek, originally called Cold Brook, the farm's namesake. The house and barn faced south, the one hundred fourteen acres running out to the Philadelphia-Pittsburgh turnpike, the road over which Lee's army made its ill-fated march to Gettysburg and within sight of the ground where Lee made his headquarters while camped near Chambersburg. Grass on the sloping rise was emerald green, sunlight falling on it as if directed from Heaven and the trees bordering the stream stood close together like lovers. The house itself was a two-and-a-half story, Colonial Revival, built of beautiful native blue-gray limestone. Striking in its architecture and extensive frontage, the house had a central section flanked on either side by slightly recessed wings. A wide carved en-

trance door with a transom was set into a portico, the roof gray
Vermont slate with a pair of dormer windows topped with jack
arches of stone. Fourteen Doric columns supported a brick-
paved colonnade that spanned the front of the house and
between the columns rested tubs of geraniums and trailing ivy. It
was magnificent and Amanda's heart still caught in her throat
every time she approached the great spreading house. She ran up
the porch steps, lifted the large iron latch securing the front door
and stepped into the entrance hall. Eager to read her letter
Amanda hurried into the sitting room and plopped down in a
chair next to the fireplace. She tore open the envelope.

The letter was much as Abby's except that Michael bemoaned
the fact that this meant a delay in their marriage plans. He
planned to apply for the fall term at school but wanted to work
the summer at the Dodge Mills on St. Simons because he could
make more money there than in Chambersburg. If all went well,
he would see her in September.

Amanda clutched the letter to her chest and closed her eyes.
This news removed a lot of uncertainty and gave some direction
to the immediate future. Tomorrow she would check into the
Children's Aid Society.

The first of August came and went with the mail bringing yet
another surprise—an invitation to the wedding of Esther
Carbaugh to Tony Peterson on October 23, 1884. This was
followed two days later with a letter from Esther asking her to
be her maid-of-honor. George would be home from Paris and he
would be the best man. Esther apologized for the short notice. It
would not be a formal wedding—she and Tony would be
married in the chapel of the Episcopal Church in Penn Hills—
with a reception at home.

Amanda was puzzled but pleased. She had met Tony when he
came to the Wilson graduation. She remembered he was in

graduate school at Princeton and still had a year to go. She did not know their romance was that serious. Was there something Esther was not telling her? She was also glad that George would be at the wedding. He had sent her several post cards from France but she had elected not to respond. Still, she would be glad to see him.

Michael had been accepted as a Junior at Pennsylvania College in nearby Gettysburg. He was due to arrive the last week of August and start school September seventh.

Amanda had seen several ads in *The Valley Spirit* soliciting funds for the Children's Aid Society and she was intrigued. When she contacted Mr. Orr he invited her to meet him in town at 148 King Street to take a tour of the facilities they had rented. So on Tuesday morning she dressed carefully in a navy blue skirt and white blouse, tied a flower-trimmed hat under her chin and pulled on white gloves.

Mr. Orr greeted her on the porch and after exchanging pleasantries led her inside. "Let me show you the first floor which we have tried to furnish like a typical home rather than an institution." He led her through a large kitchen, dining room, parlor and a small bedroom which had been converted into an office. "There are four bedchambers on the second floor," he said. "We realize it is only temporary . . . we will need larger quarters very quickly . . . but it will do to get us started. Let us go into my office and talk."

He led her into the tiny office and she sat down in a rather rickety chair in front of his desk.

"What do you think so far, Miss Kennedy?" he asked.

"It looks just like a comfortable home. It will seem like heaven to these children after being in the almshouse at the county jail." Her face grew uncomfortably warm. "I never realized that orphans were housed there."

Mr. Orr pulled at his mustache. "Most people don't, but the newspaper has done its best to make them aware and raise the funds we need. So far everything has been covered by private donations." He picked up a pair of glasses and placed them on his nose. "The county has pledged to provide each child with two suits of clothing and the Directors of the Poor will pay one dollar-seventy five cents per week per child for their care."

He removed his glasses and toyed with the stems. "The principal objective of the society is to find homes for the helpless youngsters where they will be reared to be useful citizens. Most of the children will go into fostering homes. We need a person to visit these folks and process their applications, then . . . if we place a child with them . . . we will need to visit to be certain the waifs are being well cared for. It is a volunteer position. Except for the matron and cook we cannot afford paid help at this time. Would you be interested?"

Amanda hesitated. "I wish I could say yes but I do need to secure some type of paid employment."

Mr. Orr tapped his pencil on the desk. "Your college degree gives your application a lot of weight. Perhaps we can work something out. Let me talk to the other directors and see if we can support a clerical position. He opened a drawer of his desk and pulled out a sheaf of papers. We need to process these applications as soon as possible. I'll check with the directors tomorrow and let you know."

Amanda was standing at the stove stirring a pot of chicken corn soup when she heard the echo of footsteps approaching the kitchen. Strong arms encircled her waist and Michael bent over to kiss the nape of her neck. Goose bumps raised the hairs on her arms and she dropped her spoon.

"You're home," she squealed. "Lordy, Michael, you frightened me."

"Indeed, I am." He took her by the shoulders and twirled her around to face him. His black-brown eyes crinkled with laughter. She melted at the easy flash of his smile. They kissed and kissed and only Amanda's mother rushing into the kitchen saved the soup from scorching.

Sarah gave him a generous hug. "It's good to see you, Son. Can you stay for supper?"

He inhaled deeply. "That soup smells heavenly, but I'm afraid I can't. I haven't been home yet. I came straight here. I was anxious to see my girl."

"So, I see," Sarah said with a chuckle.

"If it's all right with Amanda . . . and you . . . I can come back this evening."

This time Sarah laughed. "I can't speak for Amanda but I know her little sisters are anxious to see you."

Amanda gave him a coy smile. "We have a lot to talk about. I'm anxious to hear all about your grandmother and her plans for the hotel. I'll meet you on the back porch after dinner. Say around seven?"

"Seven it is." He kissed her mother on the cheek, then with a sheepish grin planted a kiss on Amanda's lips.

That evening Amanda was waiting for Michael on the porch off the west wing when he arrived at the back of the house astride his horse, Pharaoh. He tied the stallion to the hitching post and bounded up the steps. Her mother was sitting in a wicker rocker with young John on her lap. Erin and Eliza were snuggled on a swing on either side of Amanda. Her sisters jumped up and gave him a big hug but little John didn't remember him and huddled on his mother's lap. Michael perched on the porch railing and soon they were all chattering away, plying Michael with questions about his life on the island which sounded like magic to them. He told a funny story about the resident alligator and John listened with eyes big as saucers.

An hour later Sarah herded the children off to bed and

Michael moved from the rail to sit beside Amanda on the swing.

"I couldn't believe Papa and Abby still had Pharaoh," Michael said.

"Uncle Ford never gave up hope that you would come home," Amanda said. Michael put his arm around her and she rested her head against his shoulder. The summer twilight was filled with a cacophony of sound from the night creatures: the soft croak of bullfrogs from Falling Spring, the hoot of an owl, the pulsating whir of cicadas, and from a nearby farm the lowing of cows. Michael took a deep breath and closed his eyes. "I've missed these sounds and smells. It's different somehow. On the island you get the musky odor of the marsh mixed with the salt air. Here you smell fertilized fields and sweet grass. Both are satisfying." He pushed the swing slowly back and forth with his foot.

"I've missed you," Amanda said.

"And I've missed you. More than you know. But I'm here now and it's like starting all over."

"I really won't get to see you that much once you start school. You'll be busy trying to pick up where you left off and get back into schoolboy mode."

"Well, you know we've talked about it in our letters. You said you wanted to get a job somewhere and I'll come home as often as I can . . . it's only twenty-five miles from Gettysburg to Chambersburg. Although, you are right, it will be hard for me to start studying again. I never was a good student."

Amanda didn't confide her worries on that score. Michael had always struggled to make passing grades. Quietly, they rocked the swing and held hands. The surprising summer day had fallen asleep, twilight merging into night. Amanda was content—thinking long thoughts, happy thoughts, sad thoughts, thoughts of love and youth. In the end it was she who broke the silence. "Speaking of school . . . I've been thinking of going to nursing school."

Michael's jaw dropped.

"Nursing school? You want to be a nurse?"

"I've been thinking about it. In the meantime I'm waiting to hear about a job at the new Children's Aid Society. Dr. Susserott tends to the children when they are ill, but he has a busy practice and is active in many social organizations. There is a real need for a visiting nurse. I could attend a training school at the same time you are finishing college."

"And then what? You are going to be a nurse in Chambersburg while I run a hotel in Georgia?" A vein throbbed in Michael's temple and his face was flushed. "I thought we were going to get married. Where does that fit into your plans?"

Where indeed? Amanda swallowed dryly. "You said yourself it would take a while before you could afford to get married. That you must rebuild and get the business running first. Let me do something worthwhile with my time while I'm waiting. It's not my fault that a hurricane set us back several years."

"Now you are trying to make me feel guilty. I didn't plan the darn hurricane." He jumped to his feet causing the swing to jerk backwards. "I don't care for your idea . . . I don't care for it one little bit!"

Amanda bristled. She realized they were having their first spat. Her own anger rose to meet his. She was not going to let any man dictate what she could or could not do. She pressed her lips together. "I have already written to several training schools about their programs. I will make my decision after I learn the fee and timetable." She reached up and tugged at his hand. "Sit down, please. I don't want to fight with you, especially on your first night home. We will work things out. I can be a visiting nurse on the island as easily as in Chambersburg if that's what I choose to do. Right now it's just an idea. A dream I can't afford." She forced a smile. "The future is ours to shape in any way that will make both of us happy, Michael."

He sank down beside her and pressed his shoulder against

hers. "I'm terrified that I will lose you, Amanda," he whispered in his soft, rich baritone voice.

"You won't, dearest. I promise you that. Right now I'm unsure about a lot of things . . . about my place in the scheme of things . . . but not about my love for you."

He kissed her softly and they snuggled closely together whispering endearments. But the mood of the tranquil evening had been broken. The night creatures still stirred, there was a chorus of synchronized croaking from the banks of the Falling Spring, fireflies flashed their lights in search of a mate. But something was subtly different.

Chapter Five

ℬy October the Children's Aid Society on King Street was home to thirteen homeless children and Amanda had been hired to work four days a week processing applications.

Mr. Orr met her once more to give her a tour before outlining her duties.

"I can't tell you how happy we are to have you, my dear," he said as he greeted her in the vestibule. "Let's go right upstairs and I'll show you the sleeping arrangements." They climbed the stairs and entered a long, poorly lit hallway with two doors opening on both sides. The four bedchambers, two for boys and two for girls, were like dormitories with three-tier bunk beds, end to end, lining the walls. It was midmorning and the rooms were pristine and empty. As Amanda stood in the doorway of one of the rooms, her gaze came to rest on the floor beneath one of the bunks. A pair of small boots stood like two erect soldiers under the bedstead. They were spotless, polished to a high gloss. For some reason that tiny pair of boots tore at her heart and she felt tears burn her eyes.

Mr. Orr guided her through the rest of the home: the kitchen where a cook and several older girls were bustling about, the fenced play-yard filled with squealing youngsters, then into his small office.

Amanda toyed with the strings on her bonnet. "I keep seeing that little pair of boots in the first bedchamber you showed me."

Mr. Orr smiled softly. "They belong to Bobby Keefer. They are his prized possession. He arrived at the Almshouse with no shoes and the boots were a homemade gift from the jailer. Bobby has a harelip and was abandoned by his mother. I am afraid he is unadoptable because of his deformity."

"Oh, but maybe someone will take pity on him."

"I'm afraid not. Parents wanting to adopt are looking for the most perfect child we can offer. Even foster parents want children that will blend in and not present a physical problem." He smiled. "But then, we can always hope, can't we?"

Within days Amanda was completely immersed in the home's mission to help these friendless waifs find a loving home or be trained to enter society with an education and a skill. She was fully in charge of the program to check the credentials of families wishing to adopt or to provide foster care. There was talk that someday the society would open a hospital in Chambersburg and Amanda felt a buzz of excitement in the idea. She loved working with the children and when not busy processing an application she organized games for them in the play-yard. As fall leaves began to litter the yard Amanda laughingly taught them how to rake the leaves into huge piles and then to take belly-flops into them.

The little boy with the shiny boots had soon attached himself to her. Bobby Keefer was mischievous and a little wild, small for his age, thin, with straight nondescript hair and a face full of freckles. But he possessed long-lashed brown eyes that were true heartbreakers.

Amanda had to admit that little Bobby soon had a special place in her heart and each time the children lined up in the living room to be inspected by prospective parents she prayed someone would choose him. But no one ever did.

Late in the month Amanda was able to secure time off to attend

Esther's wedding in Pittsburgh.

On the night before the ceremony the two girls were curled up on Esther's bed exchanging confidences when Amanda questioned the surprising quickness of the marriage.

"Well, my mother is relieved," Esther admitted. "She was beginning to hear the clock tick. I am twenty-one . . . late to be finding a husband."

"Why do girls feel marriage is so important?"

"Isn't finding a husband what we all want, Amanda? Despite our education we all want the security of home and family. It's what we have been groomed for all our lives. Even going to college was a move toward finding a mate. Oh, there is talk of more freedom and equality for women but it's still just a faint stirring of unrest. Maybe full equality will come in our children's time . . . but not ours."

"I don't agree with you," Amanda said. "It's more than a mere stirring of unrest in my breast. I think women have made tremendous strides forward in the past decade. During the Civil War wives and mothers were called on to take the place of their soldier husbands. They took part in espionage, like my Aunt Abby, nursed the wounded, and took on the responsibility of running the family farms or businesses. So, after months of controlling their own affairs, women tended to rebel when their husbands returned and demanded their subservience. Just recently Wyoming and Utah have both given women the vote. Mark my words, Esther . . . the franchise will someday be nationwide."

"Then, what is it you want, Amanda? Your future has seemed to be pretty well defined. I thought you planned to marry Michael, be a good Southern wife, and raise a family . . . an agenda no different from those of the rest of us Wilson grads."

"Nevertheless, I've always felt a disquiet at that picture of a woman. I expect more from myself than just being a wife. I attended two years of preparatory school and then four years of college at Wilson for more than that." She sighed. "I do love my work with the Children's Aid Society . . . I guess that should be enough for me."

What Amanda did not mention was that she also wanted to become a person of stature. She wanted to rise above her illegitimacy. She had never talked about that to Esther—had said only that her father was a soldier killed during the civil war. She did not speak of it now. Instead she grinned and poked Esther in the ribs. "When you were in such a hurry I thought maybe you were in the family way."

Esther blushed and dropped her gaze. "No, but I'll admit we have done it."

"You didn't!"

"I . . . well, I didn't want him to look elsewhere and we were practically engaged. How about you and Michael?"

"No." She giggled. "Not yet. Not that I haven't been tempted. Did it hurt?"

"A little."

"Where do you plan to go on your honeymoon?" she asked.

"My parents have a summer cottage near Johnstown. We will go there for two weeks. You would love it, Amanda. There is a huge lake with boats and miles of hiking trails. I think I told you about it before. I haven't been there for several years."

"It doesn't sound like you. I've always seen you as a city girl."

Esther dimpled. "It isn't really, but Tony wants to go. He is trying to make points with Daddy."

"I haven't seen George. Will he be here?"

"Yes, but he had to work today so he had to miss the rehearsal. He won't get in until late tonight. He has been best man at plenty of weddings so I am sure he knows the ropes."

Amanda yawned. "We had better get to bed." She reached over and pulled Esther into her arms for a hug. "Tomorrow is your big day."

•   •   •

Following the beautiful wedding about forty people made their way to the Carbaugh's home for the reception. The guests had begun to congregate in the sitting room when George walked through the doorway and headed straight for Amanda. They had exchanged glances as they stood beside Esther and Tony at the alter but had not talked. Now, he grasped each of her hands in his fingers and raised her right hand to his lips to plant a kiss. His brown eyes sparkled with warmth and Amanda felt a tingle of pleasure.

He said something she couldn't hear. The room was a bedlam of noise, the orchestra had begun to play and loud laughter and shouts of endearment rang out. George leaned closer to her. "Come with me. The library is quieter and I want to talk to you."

He picked up two glasses of wine as they passed a waiter and led her into a room that smelled of cigar smoke and whiskey— obviously a gentleman's retreat. A long couch of soft brown leather faced the fireplace and they sank down side by side. He handed her a glass of wine and tipped his against hers. "A toast," he said, "to the renewal of a most enjoyable friendship."

"I'll drink to that," Amanda said with a grin. "Now tell me about Paris. Are you finished with your studies? Are you here for good?"

"Reluctantly, yes . . . to both questions. I wanted to be here for Esther's wedding and the trip across the ocean is too arduous and expensive to be going back and forth. But I was thoroughly immersed in the life there." He hesitated. "I hated to come home. It's hard to explain. Aside from the Paris Medicale, Paris, as I got to know her, is a composite of many worlds."

Amanda smiled. "They say it is a beautiful city."

"It is. I loved to stroll through Luxembourg Gardens and spread a blanket beneath its magnificent trees. It was a wonderful place to study. Sometimes I'd take long walks by the

Seine and spend hours just gazing at the river. But there is more to it than just the beauty of the city . . . much more. Art, music, poetry, museums, good intellectual conversation . . . Paris has it all."

"I never understood what made you decide to study abroad instead of here in America?"

"I met Oliver Wendell Holmes at a Harvard reception and was captivated by his tales of his medical years at the Paris Medicale several decades ago. He talked at length about the remarkable French physicians under whom he had once studied. At that time Paris was far ahead of America in medical training and research. Modern scientific medicine had its rise in France in the early days of this century. Why, Amanda, in one year Paris Medicale provided care for more than sixty-five thousand patients while Massachusetts General served fewer than eight hundred. And in all of France hospital care and student training was free, even for Americans. Due to what Holmes and others brought back to America the disparagement in training has all but disappeared but I was so enthralled by his stories I became obsessed with the idea of studying at the great Hotel Dieu where he trained."

"Other than the glamour do you really think the training was better?" Amanda asked.

George grinned. "Maybe not, but it was a glorious experience. I'll admit I was completely overwhelmed by everything when I first arrived. Language, of course, was a major barrier but I learned fast and soon fell in love with the excitement and intellectual challenge of the city."

Amanda wagged a finger at him. Esther had written her that her brother was living on intimate terms with a *grisette* named Olivia, a practice quite acceptable by Parisians. "I understand you had another love. What about Olivia?"

George had the courtesy to blush. "My sister talks too much," he muttered. "Now, enough about me. What have you been doing with your life since I last saw you in New York?"

"Well, I graduated in June with a Liberal Arts Degree, then I took part in a 'Right to Vote' march and I have been helping to establish a Children's Aid home in Chambersburg for the past month. I'm afraid it's nothing as exciting as your life abroad."

George's brow puckered in a frown. "I hope this doesn't mean you've become a suffragette, yielding an axe and smashing up saloons."

Amanda laughed. "I'm not that radical." She fell silent and took a sip of wine. In all honesty George's motivation—being inspired by Oliver Wendell Holmes—was little different from the influence Lavinia Dock had on her. What would George think if she confided her instinct to pursue a nursing career?

George interrupted her thoughts. "What about your marriage plans. I thought you planned to marry as soon as you finished college."

Quickly she brought him up to date on the hurricane and subsequent delay in reconstruction of the damaged hotel, of Michael's return to Pennsylvania to get his own college degree, and of their plan to wait to get married until he was established and earning a living.

"Hmm," was all George said.

"What will you do now?" Amanda asked. "Will you go to work in a hospital here in the states?"

"First I have to do my residency. I plan to go to Massachusetts General."

"What is your specialty?"

"Anatomy . . . the same as Holmes. I told you he inspired me."

Amanda finished her wine and sat the glass down with a clink. Her chin jutted as she looked at George intently. "I took a Science Course during my Senior year and thoroughly enjoyed it. Like you, I've been inspired by someone. I'm thinking seriously about studying nursing."

"Good for you. Where . . . when?"

Amanda looked surprised. "I thought you had a rather low opinion of nurses."

"I did. But in France nursing is a noble profession, probably due to the influence of Florence Nightingale and her work in the Crimea."

"I really haven't decided. Tuition is a problem. My mother works to make ends meet, although she has been dating an attorney and I am hoping that might lead to marriage and some security for her. I doubt he would take kindly to the responsibility of further education for me."

"Well, if you do decide to enter a program you could probably still get admitted to the spring term." His warm brown eyes sparkled. "I highly recommend Massachusetts General."

"I've sent for literature from Bellevue."

"Ah, yes. I remember you had quite an interest in New York. And, of course, my grandmother is there."

Amanda smiled. "At least I would know someone."

Unexpectedly the library door opened and Esther stuck her head in. "There you are . . . off to yourselves and missing all the fun." Her gaze swept the two of them sitting on the couch. "Come join us. Unless, that is, you prefer to be alone." She grinned with a smug look on her face.

Before Amanda returned to Chambersburg she visited the Pittsburgh department stores to buy Christmas gifts for the children at the home. Her job with the Society appealed to Amanda—it was a type of mission care that came to the aid of those who had neither friends nor family and who might otherwise become paupers or criminals. It was a stretch, but she could not help thinking that her widowed mother, without Aunt Abby's support, might have been left pregnant and destitute, leaving Amanda to grow up in the almshouse as some of these children had.

Esther's wedding had left Amanda restless and full of self-examination. She needed to think. She had some decisions about her future to make. So after a hectic day at the children's home where a little girl had fallen and had a severe laceration on her cheek, Amanda turned her horse and carriage north on Philadelphia Avenue toward Wilson College. The mists of late fall blanketed the campus and great ribbons of magenta-and-gold leaves floated to the earth. The dreaming beauty of the stone buildings seeped into her soul as she rumbled down the stone path to the edge of the silver snake that was Conococheague Creek. She stepped down from the carriage, draped the reins around a nearby sapling, spread her long skirts and settled her back against the rough back of a scarlet maple. Brook trout darted in and out of creek stones half-lit by shadows and leaves floated by like tiny rafts of color.

Amanda closed her eyes and allowed her thoughts to drift like the slow turn of the season on the great campus. She could almost smell the chalk and ink of classrooms, hear the giggles of young girls and the chords of the mighty organ in chapel. These memories were as golden as the leaves drifting down to settle on her lap. She knew Wilson to be atypical of the ordinary college—elitist and chauvinistic—simple and haughty, and very particular. It had left its mark on every part of her. How could it not? The knowledge gained there had been intended to direct her future as well as her past. So where did she go from here? Was she automatically destined for a life with a husband and children, a charming hostess, maybe a volunteer for a worthy charity to keep herself occupied? Would that road be fulfilling enough? That was the life Michael wanted, but she wasn't ready to surrender. Could she live her life through her husband and children? What about herself? Who was she? She recognized that she was a dreamer always yearning. Oh yes, she yearned. The problem was she could never quite put her finger on just

what she yearned for. What was her future? With Michael returning to college her marriage plans were on hold for the next
two or three years. What in the meantime? What then?

Her reverie was disturbed by a nearby fisherman who seemed
to have a trout on his line. The fish flopped and struggled,
fighting to be free. When Amanda looked at the fish, she saw
herself.

In November the Children's Aid was struck with an epidemic of
influenza. Dr. Suesserott enlisted her aid and Amanda moved
into the home to be able to nurse the sick children during the
night while the good doctor got a few hours sleep. She was
having a fresh cup of coffee for breakfast before going home to
get some sleep when John Orr came into the kitchen. "I could
use a cup of coffee," he said as he poured himself a mug of the
steaming brew. He took a sip and smacked his lips. "Ah, just the
way I like it . . . black and extra bold." He sat down and gave her
a smile. "I can't thank you enough for the help you have given
us during this crisis," he said, setting the coffee on the corner of
the table. "Dr. Suesserott tells me you are a born nurse."

"I find the work very rewarding," Amanda acknowledged.

"Have you given any thought to pursing it as a profession?"

"I have. In fact I have sent for some literature from several
nursing schools."

"Excellent. As I recall you are a Wilson graduate. That might
qualify you for a scholarship."

"I hadn't considered that possibility."

Mr. Orr lifted his coffee cup then changed his mind and
returned it to his saucer. "Check into it, my dear. As you know I
am a newspaper man and I recently read a few articles about the
movement to upgrade the training and status of nurses. Social
work, in particular, is being advanced by a Miss Lillian Wald in
New York City. I have printed several of her provocative ar-

ticles."

"Thank you, sir. I will look into it. Actually, I have read your pieces about Miss Wald and although I mentioned nursing I believe I am more interested in social work."

Mr. Orr got up and carried his cup to the sink. "The two professions go together, you know. If you are interested in social work, I suggest you concentrate on a visiting nurse program. Surely you have heard of 'Aunt Lizzie' Keagy, our local angel of mercy. She can be found every day walking our streets with a basket on her arm, filling the bodies and souls of the needy. 'Aunt Lizzie' is in her eighty-third year and her work is invaluable."

"I have seen her around town."

"Well, let me know if I can be of any help. I would be glad to give you a letter of recommendation."

•   •   •

December brought Christmas break and Michael savored every minute away from the hated books. He planned to spend every hour with Amanda. Days were crisp and cold, yet a sturdy sun brightened the sky. He loved the festive decorations and the smells of Christmas: the candles burning in every window, the scent of cinnamon and yeast in the kitchen, the wassail bowl smelling of raisins and honey. He took Amanda on sleigh rides across the open fields bordering Falling Spring Road, spooking deer and brightly plumed pheasants and once a black bear. Amanda went to his Christmas dance at Pennsylvania College and they had a romantic dinner at the beautifully decorated Hotel Gettysburg. He attended her Christmas party at the Children's Aid and helped her distribute the gifts she had bought in Pittsburgh. They ice-skated on the frozen Conococheague. Life was unfolding in a different way from the one he had envisioned. He began to wonder if his chosen path in the South was the right one.

The only cloud on the horizon was the undeniable fact that he was in danger of failing his college courses. He simply was not a student. He liked working with his hands—carpentry and masonry suited him. Books didn't. Sometimes he felt as if he were going backward instead of forward. Here he was, twenty-three years old and still in school. By now he should be married—raising a family—pursuing a career.

He and Amanda were sitting in Miller's Drug Store sipping mugs of steaming hot chocolate when he broached his current dilemma. "I know I flunked one of my finals, maybe even two. I don't think I can make it through the next semester without tutoring."

"Your grandmother will be terribly disappointed. Have you talked to your father about it?"

"Yes, and he isn't too sympathetic. He thinks I'm not trying hard enough."

"Are you?"

"I do try. I simply can't see why I have to take subjects like Ancient History and Shakespeare to build a hotel."

"But Michael there's much more involved in creating a prosperous resort than simply putting up a building. You will be meeting people from all walks of life and social standing. It's important that you be polished and educated. Your grandmother understands this . . . that's why she wants you to finish college."

Michael swirled the whipped cream atop his hot chocolate. "I guess you're right, but honey I just don't have the aptitude for book learning. I hate to ask Papa for the money to hire a tutor. I've been wondering . . . I know you are busy . . . but would you consider helping me?"

Amanda frowned. "How would we manage that? I mean you are in Gettysburg and I am in Chambersburg. Wouldn't you need help almost daily . . . for quizzes and such?"

"I think I could manage if you would just help me study for the big exams and maybe help me write my term papers when they are due." He flashed her a smile. "Of course, we could get married now and get a room in Gettysburg and be together all the time. That would solve the problem."

Amanda set her mug down with a loud clink. "That would just be the beginning of our problems. Suppose I got pregnant and you had a baby as well as a wife to support. Honestly, Michael you must be daft to even think of such a thing."

A spasm of irritation crossed Michael's face. "Sometimes I wonder just how much you do love me. I see other married students . . . some of them even have small babies . . . struggling financially, but happy just to be together. I'm getting tired of waiting. And speaking of babies I want a large family. We can't wait too much longer to get started."

"Just how many babies do you plan for us to have?" Amanda snapped.

"At least half a dozen."

"And have I no say in this?"

He saw the fire in her eyes and hesitated. "Of course, I just . . ."

"Why not a dozen?" she interrupted, her voice like ice. "What's the old saying—*keep 'em barefoot and pregnant*?"

"Now, Amanda."

Several girls at an adjacent table looked in their direction. Amanda pushed her chair back, almost knocking it over, and jumped to her feet. "I suggest we continue this conversation some other time and place."

Chapter Six

Valentines Day fell on Saturday so Michael came home from college for the weekend. Amanda was helping him with his Algebra for which he could not pass muster, but this was a special Valentines Day. He did not plan to let anything as hateful as mathematics spoil the event.

He intended to present Amanda with an engagement ring.

The pond, with its picturesque spring house, lay between Falling Spring and Garber Road and by mid-afternoon the millpond was thronged with laughing, swirling, couples. Young men and their girls held hands while gliding across the frozen ice, colorful mufflers around their necks, noses red, their breath a white mist. Displaced ducks squawked in ire as they slid across the pond trying to avoid the screeching skates. Wood smoke scented the crisp air.

Ford had a fire glowing in a large drum and had placed bales of hay in a big semicircle. As the skaters came in to warm their hands, Abby ladled mugs of hot chocolate from a large cast-iron soup kettle.

Michael could hardly wait for sundown when he planned to gather everyone around the fire to sing a few songs. He toyed with the ring, a family heirloom, deep in his pocket. Should he make a public presentation in front of their friends or wait until he and Amanda were alone. Probably the latter, although he could barely contain himself as he anticipated the look on her face when she saw the beautiful diamond.

His impatience triumphed. As the sun sank behind the barn,

the skaters formed a circle around the fire and joined hands. The cold night air rang with "Till We Meet Again." As the last notes died out Michael drew a startled Amanda into his arms. "Attention everyone," he said in a voice that trembled slightly. "This lovely girl has already promised to marry me, but on this very special night I want to present her with this ring to seal our commitment." With that he whipped the ring from his pocket and lifted her hand.

Her reaction wasn't exactly what he anticipated. He was momentarily nonplused. She had an odd look on her face and for a second he felt her pull her hand back. Then with a wan smile she let him slip the ring on her finger.

•   •   •

After the last buggy departed the pond Ford and Abby went up to the house. Amanda and Michael pulled a bale of straw close to the lingering fire and wrapped a blanket around themselves. Amanda held out her finger and the diamond caught the light of the glowing embers. Before she could ask, Michael grinned sheepishly. "It belonged to your grandmother," he admitted. "When I told Abby I wanted to buy an engagement ring, she offered it to me. She said Grandma McKenzie had left it to her to be passed on someday to a granddaughter. She wants you to have it."

"It's gorgeous."

"Yes, it is." He raised her hand to his lips and kissed her finger then folded her hand in his. "And so are you, Amanda. I'm sorry there have been so many delays. I want desperately to marry you, you know that don't you?"

"I do, and we will get married," she said. Her hand shook, her mind a whirl of conflicting emotions. Accepting this ring was a final commitment. There was no turning back now. She bowed her head unwilling to let Michael see her indecision, then with a sigh jumped to her feet and brushed straw from her skirt. "Now, let's get up to the house. I want to thank Aunt Abby for the ring."

They found Abby and Ford in the kitchen, sitting before the fireplace, the picture of contentment. Abby was knitting a sweater and Ford was reading *The Valley Spirit*. Ila and Esau, were there too—Ila had come over from Coldbrook to help with the skating party and Esau was busy filling the wood box. Amanda gave her aunt a tender kiss and thanked her for the ring, then ran over to flash her finger at Ila.

"I haven't seen that ring since your grandmammy passed," Ila said with a huge smile. "She'd be a mite pleased to see it on your finger. Esau, come here. Look at Miss Amanda's engagement ring."

Esau beamed as she held her hand out for him to see.

Ila and Esau were like family to Amanda, in fact Ila had helped deliver her while the Civil War raged around them. At that time Ila was a free servant, working for the Kennedys, and Esau was a slave—manservant to Colonial Ford McKenzie from Georgia. Esau had been freed by Ford at the end of the war but during their sojourn in Pennsylvania he had met and fallen in love with Ila. When Ford returned to marry Abby, Esau came with him and married Ila. They had five children and Esau still worked for the McKenzies at the fish hatchery while Ila now worked at Coldbrook. Esau said he had no desire to return to the South—Chambersburg was a good place to raise his family. Ila sang in the choir at AME, the African Methodist Episcopal Church, just a block from their home on Catherine Street. Chambersburg's schools were not segregated and William, his oldest boy, attended the Chambersburg Academy on Third Street and was on the baseball team.

Amanda and Michael drew up chairs in front of the fire. A log snapped and sizzled in a shower of sparks before settling on the hearth and Ford carefully added another piece of sweet-smelling apple wood. Before sitting down, Amanda gave her aunt another hug and kiss. "Thank you, thank you, thank you," she said. "Michael told me this was Grandmother Kennedy's ring."

A shadow passed over Abby's face, then she smiled. "I thought it should stay in the family. Since Molly's death I have no daughter. It should go to you."

"Well, it was very nice of you. Michael certainly surprised me."

Abby smiled at Michael and reached over to pat his hand. "You know, Son, you won't have skating parties on St. Simons."

"I know and I will miss the seasons . . . the wonderful leaf change in the fall and the snow in winter. But I love the island too. Especially the fantastic sunsets and the golden marshes. And I have grown to admire the Southern culture. It is much more laid back and . . . I don't know . . . soft, somehow."

"Refined," Ford interjected.

"Yes, and I admire Southern women. They have a certain graciousness that sets them apart, that enhances their femininity. They never seem to question their place in the home."

Amanda pursed her lips. "Michael doesn't think much of us Northern women with our causes and careers."

"I didn't say that," Michael retorted. "There's just a difference." He hesitated. "I guess my picture of a woman as wife and mother reflects my Indian culture as well."

Ford winked at Abby and she raised her eyebrows. "I think that is a weighty subject best left for another day, Ford said. "We've had a busy day. It's time for bed."

•   •   •

Profanity was only one of little Bobby Keefer's problems, but it was a huge one. He had been raised in the confines of the county jail so it was only natural that he had learned to speak the language of the criminals housed there.

It had become Amanda's mission to stop his cussing.

"Miss Mander, I hafta piss," Bobby announced as they were walking down King Street.

"Bobby *piss* is not a nice word."

"What you say then?"

Amanda realized *urinate* was too complicated for his five-year-old vocabulary so she said, "Just say you have to pee."

"What's the difference?" He reached down to grab himself. "Son-of-a-bitch I'm gonna go in ma pants iffen you don't do somethin'."

Amanda gave a deep sigh and led him behind a nearby shed. She'd worry about the language later.

After he relieved himself, they continued walking. She was taking Bobby to his first dental appointment and she could only imagine what the good dentist was in for. The child was a rogue yet he had wormed his way into her heart. He had adopted her and followed her like a shadow every minute she was at the home. She knew better than to show favoritism among the children but she worried that they sensed her partiality and were cruel to him because of it. She had bought a toy for every child at Christmas, wrapped each one in colorful paper and placed them under the tree. Bobby's was wrapped in green paper with a huge red bow and a tag with his name "Bobby Keefer" in bold black letters. He carried it around for a week without unwrapping it because he said: "I ain't never got such a pretty present and don't want to spoil the damn surprise." It was a little toy truck and he placed it beside his prized boots every night when he went to bed.

It was beginning to be clear that the present aid building was no longer functional for the society's purposes and larger accommodations were being sought. A hydrant at the back door was King Street's only plumbing and twelve more children were waiting for admittance to the home. The board had its eye on a larger property near Chambersburg's East Point.

When couples approached the society about an adoption, it was the custom for the matron to herd all of the orphans into the parlor and line them up in a row. Then the prospective parents would walk back and forth inspecting each anxious child. Amanda hated the custom and her heart broke at the disappointment on the children's faces as they were passed by. The adults were usually farmers looking for an older boy or girl to do farm work or they were childless couples eyeing youngsters barely walking that they could raise as their own. The in-betweens, or children with a deformity, hardly got a glance. Bobby was one of them.

One afternoon a man appeared at the door of the home in dirty overalls. He was a farmer, perhaps forty years old, with a long flowing beard and a scrawny neck. He said he was interested in a mature boy. The matron, a middle-aged woman with darting green eyes and a mole with a hair growing out of it on her chin, assembled the children, walking down the line, straightening their clothes or slicking back their hair. The man began to make his way down the line, pausing only before those husky boys with strong shoulders. Then for some reason he hesitated in front of little Bobby. Overcome with excitement, Bobby pushed himself forward and his twisted mouth formed a frightening grin. The man grimaced in disgust and moved quickly on. He chose a boy at the end of the line, named Henry, fourteen years old with blond hair and bulging biceps.

The matron dismissed the children and as Amanda led the farmer into the office to process the paper work she saw Bobby push one of the smaller boys to the floor and begin to pummel him, all the while shouting obscenities. He had done this once before, as a show of strength when not chosen, but this act of aggression took Amanda by surprise and she was slow to react. The matron stepped in to separate them, soon splattered by blood from the younger boy's nose. When she ultimately got them apart, Bobby flew up the stairs to his room and slammed the door. Amanda finished the farmer's paperwork, then looked up at him with a frown. "I'm wondering," she said, "why you stopped in front of the Keefer boy. He is only a small child."

"I'm sorry if I upset him. I was looking at his lip. I never saw such a thing before." The farmer twisted the brim of his hat in his calloused hands. "The child should be used to it. That shouldn't have caused him to act the way he did."

"No one likes to be reminded of a deformity," Amanda said gently. Her blue eyes filled with tears and she shuffled and reshuffled the papers on her desk. She blinked against the tears and looked at him again.

The farmer stood. "If you're finished with me, I'd like to collect my boy and leave."

Amanda also rose to her feet. "We are indeed finished, sir. Follow me." They walked into the parlor where the matron was waiting beside the smiling, excited lad. "I wish you well," Amanda said, shaking the man's hand. "You have a fine boy there . . . treat him well."

Amanda stood in the doorway watching the farmer lead Henry away, her thoughts drifting from joy to despair. Joy for the boy who had found a home and would hopefully find a loving family, despair for the one who had suffered the terrible dregs of rejection. As she walked down the hall to her office, she heard crying emanating from the room used for the little boys. She had heard this sort of crying before. It came on bad nights when the children remembered their mothers.

It started to snow the morning of March 23 and by mid-afternoon the weather had turned into a monstrous blizzard.

Roads drifted shut, wind howled down the chimney, and snow piled up above the windowsills. Ila prepared steaming teakettles of hot water to prime the pump beside the kitchen door and kept the fires going in every room.

After tucking the children into bed with extra bricks heated in the fireplace to keep them warm, Amanda and her mother drew chairs close to the fire to be snug and warm. Sarah thumbed through the latest issue of *Harper's Bazaar* and Amanda had her nose buried in a copy of *Lady's Book*, one of the most popular women's magazines of the period.

Amanda laid aside her magazine and stared into the fire.

"Mom," she said.

"What, dear?"

"I'm glad you and Mr. Wingert are thinking of getting married. You deserve some happiness. But I can't help wonder how he feels about me? Has he ever said?"

"Feel about you? I guess the same as he feels about all of you children. His former wife was unable to give him any offspring and he is tickled to have a ready-made family. Why do you ask?"

"Oh, I don't know. I just wondered if he looked at me differently. I mean . . . well, you know . . . if he remembers that I am illegitimate. If I remind him how I was conceived."

Sarah didn't answer immediately. She looked incurably sad. "We have never really talked about that terrible night. He knows, of course, probably from friends. When he asked me, I gave him the barest of details and indicated it was history I did not wish to discuss. We never spoke of it again."

"Mom. . . ."

"Yes?"

"You never gave me more than *the barest of details* either. My misbegotten status haunts me. I need to know who fathered me."

Her mother's face twisted in a grimace, then she laid her magazine aside. For the next half hour she spoke of the night when a drunken confederate soldier broke into her room and raped her. Her father had heard her screams and rushed to protect her. Tears ran down Sarah's face as she talked of the awful consequences of the ensuing altercation. During the scuffle shots were fired and her father was killed.

When Sarah finished her tale and fell silent Amanda jumped up and knelt before her mother. She threw her arms around her and they sobbed together, releasing emotions that had hobbled both of them for years. When the storm of emotion had subsided, Amanda had one more question. "Do you know the soldier's name?"

"Yes. I'll never forget it. But I do not know any more about him." Her eyes brimmed with tears. "Amanda, do not hate him. He was far from home and drunk on that god-awful whiskey. I forgave him a long time ago."

"Forgave? I find that hard to believe."

"I said I forgave him. Forgetting is another matter."

"I'd still like his name. Maybe I could find out more about my heritage. I feel like half a person."

Sarah shook her head. "Let it alone. You will only open old wounds." She picked up her magazine, an indication that the conversation was over.

Amanda sighed and rose to go upstairs to her room. At least she knew more about her genetic makeup than she had when the evening started. Carrying a candle she made her way across the spacious center hall and started up the intricately carved oak staircase to her room. She paused on the first landing to gaze through the frosted crystalline web of frost-flowers that fretted the window and thawed a space by pressing her warm hand on the glass to look out on the grounds. To the north snow blanked open farmland—silent and secluded. She would hate to leave this beautiful home but an inner voice had begun to speak of a need to move on.

She climbed the rest of the stairs and turned left to enter her bedchamber. All of the rooms at Coldbrook were the full width of the house and Amanda's room had two windows on each side for light and ventilation. A fireplace with a graceful mantle had been lit by Ila and was burning warmly. Beautiful mahogany bedroom furniture shone faintly in the dim room. A chiffonier and two wooden chairs flanked the fireplace on its right and a comfortable easy chair with a reading table and an oil lamp was on its left. The room was papered above the chair rail that circled the room and a braided rug warmed wood-pegged floors. She loved this room—had grown up here. Amanda undressed, donned a heavy flannel nightdress and climbed into the four-poster rice bed centered on the south facing wall. The clouds had cleared and moonlight slanted through frosted windows where a thousand stars twinkled in the cold, crisp night sky. She lay thinking about what her mother had said. And not said.

Chapter Seven

The years passed quickly. It was now July 1888. The Children's Aid Society moved to larger quarters twice before they raised enough money to buy property on Federal Hill. The stately mansion, overlooking North Franklin Street at Pleasant Street, would remain its home for eighty-eight years.

With Amanda's tutoring help Michael graduated from college and was back at St. Simons working feverishly on the hotel. During his two years in Chambersburg he had returned each summer to his old job with P. Nichols Furniture and saved every penny to put into the reconstruction. His grandmother had not yet sold her home in Savannah, but she did sign a note for the funds he needed to rebuild. Michael planned to have the hotel open by the 4th of July next year for the summer tourist trade.

Amanda's mother and Peter Wingert were now married. While it would break Amanda's heart to leave Coldbrook staying felt like an imposition. It was time for her to move on. After all, she had been away at school for four years and hardly knew Peter. She needed to become independent.

At the quarterly meeting of the Children's Aid Society, held at Wilson College, Amanda found herself seated beside one of the directors, Amos Woodstock. As they waited for the meeting to begin they fell into easy conversation and Amanda revealed that she was a recent graduate of the college. Mr. Woodstock immediately became interested. He was looking for a tutor for his nineteen-year-old daughter, Silvia, who would be entering her senior year at Wilson and was having problems with her grades. Would Amanda be interested?

She certainly would. Since the Woodstock home was on Ragged Edge Road and rather far out of town, compensation included room and board. That would be perfect. Silvia was not boarding at the college so Amanda arranged to meet her at her home on Saturday afternoon.

Amanda left the meeting deep in thought. This position would give her the opportunity to move out of Coldbrook with no hard feelings. In addition it would give her extra income which she could certainly use. She needed a few notions in town so she took a shortcut across the college grounds, then through an alleyway to Broad Street. It was a lovely summer afternoon with blue skies and fluffy white clouds. She strolled leisurely, stopping at Mary Morrow's front lawn to admire a large hydrangea bush with a huge cluster of violet blooms. She bent over to cradle one on the blossoms in her hand inhaling deeply. When she straightened up a small "Room to Let" sign in one of the windows caught her attention. *What a lovely place to live*, she thought. She tucked the image away in her mind. *What a shame the Woodstock's didn't live here instead of miles out of town.*

On Saturday Amanda borrowed Peter's carriage and headed west on the turnpike to Ragged Edge Road. She rode past several large farms with acres of sorghum and fields of corn just coming into a tassel under a high overhead sun. She flipped open the cover of the gold pocket watch she wore on a chain around her neck to check the time. It was taking longer than she had expected. She pursed her lips. The Woodstock farm was further out of town than she remembered. At long last she rounded a bend and saw it on her right. The setting was spectacular. The home sat regally atop a wooded knoll, back from the narrow road named for a large outcropping of rock on the northwest corner of rolling countryside. It was lovely—three stories high with yellow stucco walls on a foundation of Pennsylvania fieldstone, the fieldstone repeated on numerous chimneys rising from a sharply pitched roof. Sheep grazed tranquilly on rolling fields of green that fell away to the Conococheague and a copse thick with oaks and hemlocks.

Amanda tied the horse to a hitching post at the side of the house and stepped up to a wide veranda that wrapped around the front of the home and ran along one side. She breathed deeply of air fresh from pine and a recent rainfall and she thought she could hear the rush of water from the nearby creek.

The front door opened and Mr. Woodstock stepped out.

"Welcome to Ragged Edge."

"Thank you. What a lovely place."

"We enjoy it. Come in. Come in. Silvia is anxious to meet you." He ushered her into the house through a door that led directly into an impressive entry from which a beautifully carved staircase spiraled upward.

"Everyone is waiting in the drawing room," he said as he led her into a large, bright room with long windows facing a terrace that ran down to the creek. Two sofas faced each other in front of a walk-in fireplace and two ladies, apparently Mrs. Woodstock and her daughter, sat on one of them smiling at her.

"I told Silvia why you are here," he said, introducing them to Amanda. He smiled at his daughter. "She'll cooperate although she isn't entirely happy with the idea that she needs a tutor. But she understands and desperately wants to stay and graduate from Wilson." He pushed his wire-framed spectacles up the bridge of his nose. "Both Mrs. Woodstock and I are entirely in favor of the arrangement."

"Please sit down," Mrs. Woodstock said.

Amanda settled herself on the second sofa and they were soon talking easily, getting to know each other and discussing her years at the college. Silvia listened avidly. She was of average height, with gray-green eyes and flaxen hair that hung straight around an oval face. Otherwise quite ordinary looking she had a shy smile and a dimple that made up for her nondescript features.

A maid served tea and blueberry scones, Amanda explained how many hours they would spend studying and what help she could provide for term papers.

"Good. Good." Mr. Woodstock said. He shot Silvia a smile. "Why don't you give Amanda a tour of the house?"

Silvia led the way up the staircase of fine-grained chestnut, lit by a stained glass skylight, to the second floor bedrooms. "My bedroom is at the end of the hall," she said, "and the servants quarters are in the attic under the gables." They passed a closed door. "It's really a rather small house. I guess that would be your bedroom if you decide to stay with us. It's my brother's room but he is married now." Amanda frowned and said nothing. She was already having some second thoughts about traveling so far.

"Daddy said we could use his office on the first floor for a schoolroom. Do you want to see my bedroom?"

"Thank you. I'm sure it is quite lovely."

After viewing her room they returned to the parlor where Mr. and Mrs. Woodstock were waiting. Her father rose and led Amanda back to the sofa. "Well," he said, "Mother and I have discussed your credentials and would like to offer you the position. What do you think?"

"I would be honored to accept." She bit her lip with a sudden stab of anxiety. "But I don't own a carriage and I must maintain my position at the Children's Aid. Your home is quite a distance from town. I'm afraid room and board as compensation would be impractical."

Mr. Woodstock cleared his throat and looked at his wife. She gave him a slight nod.

"Can you tutor Silvia at the college?"

"I think that can be arranged." She remembered the "To Let" sign at the Morrow house. "If not, I could do it in my room."

"Then I believe we can arrive at satisfactory terms. Silvia, are you in agreement with our hiring Miss Kennedy to provide you with the tutoring you need?"

"Yes, Daddy," she said. She blushed and added, "We have already become friends."

For the next half hour they discussed terms and the course of study, then the niceties dispensed with, Amanda returned to town and went immediately to the Morrow house across from the college.

The Morrow's Gothic style house with its steeply pitched roof, cross gables, deep overhangs, fretwork and tall windows looked like something out of a Grimms Fairy Tale. A tower rose from the left side of the house with a charming "chimney pot" topped by a star. An ancient oak tree shaded the manicured lawn, geraniums spilled from terrace pots, and a purple-flowered clematis vine climbed a narrow trellis. The lovely olive-green home struck a chord in Amanda's heart. *I want to live here*, she thought as she walked up the wide front porch steps and knocked on the door. *This house says home.*

She was told the room was still available and was led by a housemaid to a small hallway at the rear of the house.

"This door opens to a path leading to the college and gives you more or less a private entrance to the bedrooms upstairs," the maid said. They walked back to the front hall and climbed the fairly wide staircase that turned right at the top and led to the available room. It was a bright, good-sized chamber showing papered walls and a carpeted floor. Three tall windows, set side by side, formed a bay dressed with pristine white muslin curtains. Late afternoon light slanting through the glass made dust motes shimmer and edged the room in gold. Amanda drew a deep breath of delight.

A French Victorian bedstead with a matching rosewood bureau, graced one wall. Two Boston rockers sat in front of the windows, separated by a marble-top table containing a basin and large-mouth pitcher for washing. A slant-top desk with a Hitchcock chair was angled across one corner. She would need another chair if she was to teach in this room but she could bring one from home. The wallpaper was a green ivy pattern and Currier and Ives prints adorned the walls. It was altogether lovely.

"I am definitely interested," Amanda said to the waiting servant. "May I ask the rent?"

"You will have to talk with the lady of the house about that. I'll show you to the sitting room and summon her."

After an intensive interview with Mrs. Morrow discussing house rules and the expected rent Amanda was furnished with a key to the room. Now, the only thing left to do on this exciting day was to go home and tell her mother that she was striking out on her own.

In August Amanda received a letter from Esther inviting her to spend a weekend with her family at their cottage on Lake Conemaugh near Johnstown. She was thrilled—she hadn't seen Esther for six years, nor her little girl. Of course, she would go. After arranging for a suitable time in October she took a train to Johnstown where the train stops before beginning the long climb up the Alleghenies to Altoona. Esther met her at the station.

Fall in the mountains—it was fantastic. The Conemaugh and Stoney creek dashed and plunged along rocky channels, down steep mountain sides robed in dark green hemlock and spruce. Maples, just beginning to show color, vied with yellow goldenrod and purple-red sumac and Virginia creeper.

Esther chattered away, giving Amanda a running commentary on their surroundings. "Johnstown was founded by Joseph Johns, a German settler. Before that it was an Indian village called Kickenapawling. Like Pittsburgh, river traffic gave it its beginning. The Conemaugh River at the end of town was the navigational head for the wagons piled high with merchandise from seaboard cities headed for western markets. There was also great portage from the Juniata to the Conemaugh by way of the Kittanning Trail and the Frankstown Turnpike." Esther waved her arms. "As you can see, Johnstown is a busy, industrious steel town. Most of the people in the valley work at Cambria Iron and Steel Company and live along the river banks in those frame company houses. But most of the wealthy mill and railroad executives live up in the mountains away from the creeks which flood every spring."

Esther turned the carriage up a steep road that followed the western shore of a tumbling mountain stream leading to the lake. It was a steep climb but once they left the smoke and acrid smell of the steel mill the mountains became breathtaking—the air clean and sweet-smelling, the green, densely forested hills and mountain streams strewn with sun-drenched boulders. Twenty miles up Conemaugh Creek, beyond the workingmen's villages of South Fork and Mineral Point, Esther turned the carriage across a gravel road atop the dam restraining Conemaugh Lake. She stopped so Amanda could take in the full splendor of the emerald body of placid water.

"It was a small natural lake before the dam was built," Esther said, "part of the disused Pennsylvania Canal system, three hundred feet above the level of Johnstown. The dam greatly increased the little lake, and near the reservoir the Pennsylvania Railroad built a private summer resort for its employees. Our club, called the South Fork Fishing and Hunting Club, was organized some years ago, and got the use of the lake from the Pennsylvania Company. Most of the members, like Daddy, live in Pittsburgh and are prominent iron and coal men or officials of the railroad. The club added to the size of the dam, which increased the size of the lake to three miles in length."

The carriage trundled on along the shoreline and Amanda

gasped in surprise. The lake was truly beautiful—an irregular oval in shape—reflecting the fall colors of sour gums turned blood-red—shimmering in the afternoon sun. She turned to look over her shoulder at the valley below. "It seems we have been coming straight up the mountain from Johnstown. I'd hate to think what would happen if this dam ever broke," she commented.

Esther nodded. "A lot of the people in town have worried for years that it might happen. But daddy says the dam is perfectly safe." She frowned. "My engineer husband disagrees. There are a lot of leaks in the dam and he says the overflow is not large enough in times of storm to carry the surplus water away."

"Then let's hope it doesn't rain."

They turned off the breastwork and began to follow a road skirting the shoreline, past fancy trim homes with neat lawns and well-tended flower beds. All of the cottages had boardwalks leading to boathouses. Esther referred to the homes as cottages but *cottage* was hardly the word Amanda would have used to describe the elegant homes fronting the lake.

"I can't wait to throw a line in," Amanda said. "I assume the fishing is good."

"Catfish, bass, mullets, walleye, sunfish . . . you name it," Esther assured her as she turned into a driveway before a brightly painted two-story *cottage*.

The screen door flew open and a small child ran out. "Mommy, Mommy, Mommy," she screamed as she ran down the driveway, followed closely by her anxious father. He grabbed her and swung her up in his arms before she could reach the carriage." Gail, we've told you time and time again not to scream and scare the horses," he scolded.

Gail stuck out her lip and narrowed her eyes. "Mommy went away."

"Yes, and now she's back and she brought a friend to see you," Tony said.

Amanda and Esther stepped down from the carriage and Tony wound the reins around a hitching post. Esther took her little girl by the hand. "Say hello to Amanda."

"'Lo."

"Hello."

Esther lifted Gail in her arms and gave her a hug and a kiss. "Have you been a good girl for Daddy?"

"No."

Amanda laughed. The child was beautiful, the picture of Esther with blond ringlets and hazel eyes, but the resemblance ended there. A bow in her hair dangled precariously, one shoe was untied and her mouth was streaked with jelly.

Tony looked at Amanda with chagrin. "I was supposed to keep her clean but I'm afraid I failed miserably," he said.

"She's adorable anyway."

"You ladies go inside. I'll take the horse to the barn."

They climbed the wooden steps to the porch and entered a sprawling great room with a walk-in fireplace of massive native stone. The floor was pine, covered with Navajo rugs dyed in every color of the rainbow. Comfortable couches and arm chairs were scattered throughout the room and sturdy chairs were grouped around tables, inviting cards and board games. A small fire burned in the fireplace bathing the room with warm yellow light.

By evening Gail had firmly claimed Amanda as her "auntie" and refused to let go of her hand.

Maybe motherhood isn't so bad, after all, Amanda thought as she cuddled the little girl in her arms and returned Esther's delighted wink.

Tony left before dawn to hunt. That afternoon Esther suggested they walk up to the clubhouse and take advantage of the warm sunny day on its porch. They followed a boardwalk that led from the cottages through a wooded glen to the North Fork clubhouse. It was a long sprawling building—really an oversized hotel with a large dining room and a long front porch facing the lake. Wrapped in plaid blankets, with a drink and book in hand, the girls settled themselves on steamer chairs. Gail had joined a group of slightly older children who were teaching her how to play croquet.

Except for a few employees who lived at the clubhouse and two tables of women playing bridge, the clubhouse was deserted. "Most of the men are hunting," Esther said. "It will be busy this evening when they come in from the woods. Tony said he would join us here for dinner." She smiled. "Unless, that is, he has a deer to skin out."

"What do the men hunt?" Amanda asked.

"There is an open season on black bear and wildcat, but mostly they hunt deer, pheasant, ruffled grouse, and wild turkey. I think it is a barbaric sport."

Amanda drained her glass and sat it down on the table with a rather loud thunk. She squinted at Esther. "What is in these drinks? I think I feel a slight buzz."

Esther laughed. "Just enough to make you comfy. By the way, when George heard you were coming up this weekend he tried to get away but he was on call and couldn't get a substitute. He always asks about you."

Amanda felt herself blush and looked away. She opened her book. "I've been anxious to read this," she said, hopefully ending the conversation.

Tony returned empty handed from his hunt and joined them early for dinner at the club. Little Gail insisted on sitting next to "Aunty Manda" which required getting her settled on a pile of pillows.

Amanda glanced at Tony, "I would like to go fishing in the

morning, if you have an extra rod at the cottage."

"Indeed we do. I'll get a rod and reel out for you as well as a tackle box that has any kind of lure you might want. I feel sure you'll have more luck than I did today. I'd go with you, the lake is well stocked, but I want to get out in the woods early."

"Isn't it unusual to find such a large lake on the top of a mountain?"

Tony frowned. "It is manmade and as far as I'm concerned a danger to the valley below. The people in Johnstown are afraid of it. No one can see the immense height of that artificial dam built of nothing but shale, clay and straw . . . more than a hundred feet high . . . without fearing the tremendous power of the water behind it."

Esther nodded in agreement. "Tony is an engineer, you know. He has tried, and failed, to get the local authorities to inspect the last repair work done on the dam."

Tony smiled at Amanda. "You don't strike me as a fisherman. Can you bait the hook and gut the fish?"

"Absolutely."

"Then good luck. I'll look forward to fish for dinner to-morrow night."

Amanda was out early the next morning to pick out a spot on the bank of the beautiful lake. She settled herself on a little camp stool, readied her pole and threw her line in the water. Slowly she began to relax, to feel the magic of the mountains and the lake. She gave a deep sigh and let her gaze wander across the tranquil lake. Right now her life seemed to be in limbo. Dozens of issues nibbled at the edges of her mind. But water had always brought her solace, whether stream or river. She would enjoy living by the ocean with Michael. She closed her eyes and let her thoughts drift. She loved him and she did want to be with him. A sudden tug on her line interrupted her meditation and for the next hour she was busy, pulling in two large-mouth bass and a number of good-sized pan fish. More than enough for a nice meal. Happy and relaxed she returned to the cottage.

The weekend flew by all too quickly and it was with reluctance that she packed for the return to Chambersburg. Winter would soon be upon them. Michael wrote that reconstruction on the resort was going well, but he missed her terribly. She walked to the window to draw the shade and took one final look at the sun sparkling on the tranquil lake. Without warning a cloud cast an ominous shadow over the scene, darkening the water. She felt a sudden chill and shivered with a premonition that she would never look out upon this beautiful mountain lake again.

Chapter Eight

During the Georgia winter Michael rushed to finish McKenzie Resort with his grandmother's financial help. It was now nearly complete. It had been a long, lonely process and at first he was terribly homesick for Pennsylvania, especially for Amanda. But circumstances had delayed construction. He was deeply in debt and in no position to marry until the hotel was established. And so he waited.

In the spring Amanda, Abby and his father, arrived to help with a few last minute chores and offer suggestions before the grand opening of the hotel, now only months away.

Michael met the ferry at the mill dock during a rain squall and hurried to assure everyone that the storm showed no sign of becoming a hurricane. "These storms pass over quickly," he said. "Within an hour the sun will be out and our beautiful island will show you all its glory."

Amanda rolled her eyes. "I certainly hope so. The trip from the mainland was quite choppy and rocked the boat about like a bobber on my fishing line." She turned her pale face up to smile at him softly. "It was worth it, though, to see you again."

Michael put his arm around her and hugged her tightly, then turned to kiss his stepmother on the cheek and shake Papa's hand. "It's so good to see you all. I'll admit I've been homesick. But, I'm anxious to show you all what I have done."

"*You all?*" Abby said with a laugh. "I think my boy is becoming a truc Southerner."

"I can't wait to see everything," Ford said. "I'm amazed at the activity here. The lumber mill has expanded in all directions. Business seems to be thriving."

Michael beamed with pride. "Twenty ships were counted at the wharf just last week, many of them from England. They're a great boon to our expected tourist industry, Papa. St. Simons is being transformed from a small port into a grand resort area. Mr. Dodge—who owns the mill—has seen the potential. He bought up two hundred acres along the beach, divided it into plots and is selling the sites for summer cottages. Several more boats have been pressed into operation to ferry passengers from mainland Brunswick to the island. I look for business to be solid all summer as tourists swarm to our beautiful beaches."

They waited for the squall to pass, then the four of them climbed aboard a one-horse shay for the short journey from one side of the island to the other. Michael directed the horse over a lovely shell road, through woods of gigantic oaks, thickets of myrtle and magnolia, and hanging draperies of jasmine. Michael drove slowly so they could admire the full beauty of the island: glittering evergreens of various tints bound together by trailing garlands of wild jasmine whose tiny golden cups exhaled a perfume like heliotrope. Underneath it all spread the spears and fans of a palmetto and sago palm. But the pièce de résistance was the azaleas. Michael watched Amanda's eyes grow wide with wonder as she beheld bush after bush of the wild blossoms in every shade of coral and red. He grinned. "March is our most beautiful month of the year," he said. "I think this entire island becomes one gigantic azalea. Wait until you see the entrance to McKenzie Groves. James planted the azaleas when we first started to work on the grounds and they withstood the hurricane."

With a grand flourish Michael turned the horse and buggy into the lane leading to the hotel. The McKenzie plantation of over one hundred acres was situated on the southeast portion of the island, flanked on the west by vast flats of salt marshes and on the east by the ocean. They entered the grounds through a side gate where a flowering pomegranate on a trellis formed a perfect arch giving the tropical effect Michael was striving for.

Everyone gasped at the beautiful clumps of flowers lining both sides of the road.

"I never saw azaleas with such large blossoms," Abby exclaimed. "They are twice as big as those we have in the North."

"They're native to the island," Michael said. He waved his arm. "And now here's the hotel."

He saw Amanda's jaw drop when she turned to look at the imposing new structure he had managed to create and his chest swelled with pride. After the hurricane he had added ten additional rooms to the main three-story tabby dwelling. It was surrounded on three sides by a twelve foot wide veranda more than one hundred fifty feet long. Twelve fluted columns supported the veranda roof and bougainvillea climbed those on each side. The porch was lined with white rocking chairs where guests would have an unobstructed view of the ocean.

He took Amanda by the hand and led her through the front door into the lobby. It had been decorated extravagantly for their arrival. Boughs from fruit laden sour orange trees hung from the bay window. Sago leaves, palmettos, holly with beautiful red berries, and English ivy stretched across the lintel above the folding doors which divided the parlor from the dining room. The room, and all the rooms of the hotel, had been completely refinished in beautiful Georgia early pine—the choicest lumber from the hundreds of thousands of feet sawed at the St. Simons Mills.

"It's like walking into fairyland," Abby exclaimed.

"I'll admit I had help with the decorating. A young girl from the village is studying design and she did most of it."

Amanda raised her eyebrows. A young girl? She hadn't heard

about that.

Ford walked over to one of the long, deep-set windows looking out on the lawn and the beach beyond. "The grounds are beautiful, Michael. It looks like you are building a new barn, too."

"Yes, sir. We're still working on the outbuildings . . . the barn, smokehouse and servant's houses. And the grounds need a lot of work. We left that for last. James has been busy planting fruit trees. We have fig, orange, lemon, and olive."

"Olive trees?" Abby said.

"Yes. Believe it or not, olive oil has become a profitable export from the island."

His father walked over and put his hand on Michael's shoulder. "You've done a magnificent job, Son. I'm very proud of you."

Michael stood tall and breathed deeply.

Ford smiled. "Let's take a walk. I want to see the grounds and especially the beach."

While the women went upstairs to admire guest rooms, Ford and Michael walked out the French doors onto the new veranda and down the steps to the lawn. Slowly they strolled around the grounds of the old ancestral home. "I believe it's the trees and foliage that make St. Simons so beautiful . . . the twisted cedars, the flowering magnolias and the live oaks draped in Spanish Moss," Ford commented. "And I'm glad to see you stayed with tabby when you made the addition to the main dwelling."

"Well, tabby is native to the island and has withstood both war and hurricane."

They walked in silence down to the hard-packed sand beach, two hundred yards wide and running two miles north and south. The tide was halfway in and lazy surf curled at their toes. When Michael turned to direct a question to his father, he noticed Ford bring out his handkerchief to dab at eyes liquid with tears.

"Are you all right, Papa?"

Ford looked incurably sad. "This splendid beach brings back memories of a painting I once did of your mother. I can see her now, her skirt billowing in the air, her beautiful wind-blown hair, black as a raven's wing, floating about her shoulders. I fell in love as I painted her."

Michael did not know what to say. There were so many questions he had about his mother, but his father had shown no desire to talk about his life with her.

"I never saw that painting," Michael said. "Do you still have it?"

"No. The last time I saw it, it was hanging above the mantle in the parlor. That was before the Union soldiers set fire to the house." Ford's eyes were desolate. "Have you no memories of her at all?"

"I only remember that mother's hair and eyes were very dark. That is why I always assumed she was the source of my Indian blood."

"No. Cerise was French. Her maiden name was Descartes."

They strolled, shoulder to shoulder, on sand hard and level as a floor. Michael no longer felt the overpowering anger that had caused him to reject and lash out at Ford when he learned that he was illegitimate, that Ford was not his biological father. He remembered Ford's confession when he eventually told him the truth. His mother was already pregnant when she married him. She had betrayed him into thinking he had fathered her child but Michael's features soon made his true heritage apparent. Michael was three when the war ended and his mother died. It was then that Ford took him north and married Abby.

The tide was almost in, the surf more insistent, and their mood turned to laughter when a sneaky wave soaked their shoes and trousers.

"We had better get back to the house before they send out a search party for us," Michael said.

Side by side they strolled back to the hotel. "I remember that chinaberry tree," Ford remarked as they passed a tall shrub-like tree with unusual purplish, red bark. "In the spring it has long, fragrant, lilac-like flowers. Your mother always had a vase of them in the vestibule. I think you'll find a heart with our initials, carved into the tree trunk."

"I already did," Michael admitted with a grin.

Supper that night was White Terrapin Stew, a dish that Matilda was adept at making and that promised to be on the hotel's dinner menu.

"This stew is marvelous," Abby said smiling at Matilda who was hovering nearby, a serving ladle in hand.

"Ah . . . thank you, Miz Abby. I 'preciates it."

The windows were open, the air scented with the heady fragrance of camellias overlaid with the tang of salt from the ocean beyond. Abby was helped to another serving. "I seem to remember that Ford talked a lot about the rambling roses on the stone walls surrounding his home," she said to Michael. "Are they still there?"

Michael shook his head. "Nope, the hurricane took them all out, but if you like roses you should see Rose Cottage. It's the home of Mrs. Anson Dodge, wife of the mill owner and the mother of the rector at Christ Church. Mrs. Dodge has thousands of roses of all kinds." He smiled at his stepmother. "I'd love to replant a rose garden on the east lawn. Maybe you could get one started for me while you are here."

"I'd be glad to Michael."

"At the back of the grounds James has planted a long hedge of Spanish Bayonets. You all must see them. They're not only beautiful with long wavy flowers but they present a thicket so dense that it's practically animal proof."

"What kind of animals?" Amanda asked with wide eyes.

"Oh, wild boars, deer, alligators."

"Wild boars?"

Michael chuckled. "Boar hunting is a popular sport here on the island."

Ford laughed. "Enough Michael, you'll scare the women." He turned to Abby. "We must visit Jekyll Island while you are here. You didn't see it when we visited before. There's a legend that one hundred years ago St. Simons and Jekyll Island were so close together that conversations could be carried on from one island to the other. Beach erosion is given as the reason for the present two-mile stretch of water between them."

"I heard you mention a place called Jewtown when we were starting across the island," Amanda commented. "Why is it called Jewtown? It sounds out of place."

"Sig and Robert Levinson, from Brunswick, built a store down the road about a mile from the lumber mill and conducted a general merchandise business. A few houses sprung up around the store and the settlement was named Jewtown in honor of its founders."

"Hmm."

Conversation drifted to the length of their stay, the grand opening set for the fourth of July, and what each could do to help. Michael couldn't keep his eyes off Amanda. He watched the emotions cross her face as she talked about her experiences in Johnstown. Maturity had brought a strength and purpose she had lacked as a child. Tonight she wore blue calico that brought out the blue-violet of her eyes and her hair was styled differently. The fringe of bangs was gone and her long hair was fashioned into a bun at the nape of her neck. Though small, she had a well-developed body and he had an immediate reaction when he found his eyes lingering longer than they should on the swell of her full breasts. He squirmed in his chair feeling the heat rise in his face. He desperately wanted time alone with her, but he realized everyone was exhausted from their long trip and wanted to retire early.

•   •   •

The next morning Amanda jumped out of bed just before dawn, refreshed and eager for the day. She wanted to see the sun come up so she wrapped a light afghan around her night dress, ran down the stairs, slipped out to the veranda and settled into one of the rockers strategically placed for guests to view the ocean. The chairs were wet with dew, but she was determined not to miss the sunrise.

It was a cloudless morning, perfect to watch the sun rise. The stars had disappeared in a sky turning from ebony to smoky gray. Amanda could discern white caps on the inky water as the sky began to show light. The first thin edge of sun rose up out of the ocean as she watched the day ending the night. Soon crimson and lilac pinked the sky. It was an awesome beauty, like a painting made just for her and she closed her eyes in delight.

She turned at the sound of the front door whispering shut. Michael. His lips twitched with a smile when he saw her. Without a word he pulled a rocker next to hers and took her hand in understanding silence. The rising sun cast light upon morning cobwebs veiling the grass as they watched the birth of a new day.

"You've changed," he said.

"Really? How?"

"I don't know. I think . . . I guess . . . my little tomboy has turned into a lady. One I hardly recognize."

"I hope you aren't disappointed."

"Not at all." He grinned mischievously. "In fact I'd like to pull that blanket off you and ravish you on the spot."

"Michael!"

"Maybe just a kiss then?"

"No. Heavens, I'm still in my nightclothes. If people see us kissing, what will they think?" Her fingers clutched the blanket in mock terror as she fought to hide a smile.

"Don't be frightened," he said with a chuckle. "I never ravish women and I'm not going to start this time of the day . . . and against your wishes to boot." His strong fingers squeezed hers and he raised her hand to kiss her palm. "But tonight will be a different story. Promise you'll meet me here on the porch . . . alone . . . after dinner. We have many things to talk about. I want to set a wedding date and I ache to hold you in my arms."

"I promise."

"Now you had better scoot inside and get dressed before your aunt and uncle come downstairs or we will both be in serious trouble."

The day passed quickly. Abby went to visit Mrs. Dodge at Rose Garden, Michael and Ford caught the mail boat *Ruby* to Brunswick to arrange for the final inspection and disbursement of bank funds for the hotel and Amanda busied herself placing freshly ironed linens in the guest rooms.

That evening, with knowing looks, Ford and Abby retired early and Michael suggested that he and Amanda take a walk on the beach.

Amanda agreed. "I started the day watching the sunrise, I'd like to watch the sunset. Meet me on the beach in half an hour, I want to change into my bathing suit. I bought one of the new, shorter suits when I was in New York and I'm anxious to wear it. Maybe we could take a moonlight swim."

Michael's heart soared. That certainly sounded promising.

Half an hour passed before he spied her silhouette walking along the surf. This was a sunset that combined all of the features that tended to make a sunset perfect: enough clouds to allow perfect coloring and absolute quiet on the island with a sparkling flood tide covering the golden marsh grass behind them.

He ran across the broad lawn, full of such strong anticipation he felt like a drunken sailor. He also had a new swim suit, a prominent blue and white stripe with a half-sleeve top and long shorts that came just below his knee. He felt quite dapper. He did not slow until he reached Amanda then he whipped his arms around her and swung her in the air. Her hair flew against his face, her face bubbled with laughter. Tears glistened in her blue eyes. "Oh, Michael. I have been thinking of this moment all day. I've missed you so."

"Not as much as I've missed you." Michael's gaze traveled up and down her body. It was the first time he'd seen her legs—the new bathing dress and bloomers came only to her knees. She looked adorable, the navy suit had a nautical look, the blouse being fashioned after a sailor's middy blouse. He pulled her to him, her head rested on his chest and he could feel the beat of her heart. She sighed and her soft breath grazed his throat like a caress. He was desperate to kiss her. She raised her head and he lowered his. Their lips met and white heat flamed. He lowered her to the sand so they would get a better fit—his lean body pressed hard against her ample chest. She dug her fingers into his hair and held on tightly. They kissed again and again. The sun set and neither noticed. The intensity of their kisses rocked him. Amanda, too, if he read her reaction correctly. He began to slip his fingers beneath the top of her bathing suit. "No," she mumbled, but he silenced her with another kiss, touching his tongue with hers. He couldn't get enough of her, the taste of her, the smell of her, the feel of her body against his. It was as if the ocean had swallowed them and they clung together not wanting to move. He couldn't have let go even if swept by a wave. There was only now—no more waiting for an unknown future. His hand moved until he encountered a warm breast. He cupped it in his hand and caressed the nipple. She moaned with pleasure and he kissed with more passion than he knew he possessed. His reaction to her intensified. Now kissing was not enough, he couldn't kiss her deeply enough or long enough to get his fill.

Amanda was reacting the same way. Her hands moved over him, exploring him, touching his erection.

Michael was surprised. He had expected to be the leader, he had some experience in this. He had always thought his first time would be with his wife but peer pressure at college plus the long absences from Amanda had made him eager to know a woman.

All thought vanished as his body moved against Amanda's. For only a moment her hand pushed him away. "We should wait," she said, her mouth trembling.

"We can't. Oh, my darling, we will be married soon. I am a man . . . full of needs. I cannot wait any longer."

Amanda wanted to know love. She did not want to assign words to what was happening. Was she so wrong to want her first time to be without dispute? They were all but married. She had waited long enough. Her hands moved over him, hungry to feel all of him. He had shrugged off the top of his suit and she ran her hands over his hairy, muscular chest. She reclined on her back, frantic now for fulfillment.

She lifted her arms, fumbled at the back of her neck, then let her hair tumble to below her shoulders. Her chin jutted, and with a look of pride in her eyes, she gave herself to him.

The next morning it began to rain. Raindrops pattered the roof as Amanda lay abed thinking about her love for Michael. She was a woman now. The echo of last night brought a flush of heat to her face. Yet, there was a strange stirring, always that yearning for something more. What was wrong with her?

As a child she was filled with dreams of the great things she would do when she grew up. She had fought hard for permission to attend college and had achieved that goal. She had thrown herself whole heartily into work at the Children's Aid while she waited for Michael to finish his education and return to the island to fulfill his dream. Now, she felt disappointed and frustrated at the future that lay before her. She did love Michael, as much as she could love anyone; and she did want to become his wife and a mother. But . . . but there should be more. She felt disenchanted at the sex act itself. The dime novels she was so fond of reading talked of rockets going off, of glorious release and unimaginable joy. It hadn't been quite like that. She lay listening to the rain on the roof as tears stole down her cheeks. She and Michael had lain on the beach for hours talking of the future. She remembered his pleasant, open countenance creased in confusion when she spoke of a career, political rights, the opportunity for women to shape the major decisions of society. He had looked bewildered when she mentioned an interest in social work. It was not ladylike, he said. She need aspire to nothing more than being a good wife and mother. The voices of tradition said that should be fulfilling enough for a woman.

She felt the warm, fuzzy feeling of contentment slip away. Was she ready for marriage? Was she leading Michael on? Oh, God, what did she really want?

Chapter Nine

*B*ack in Chambersburg Amanda lay wide awake. Once more she faced a night of decisions.

Friday's edition of Chambersburg's *The Valley Spirit* lay open nearby, headlines seeming to scream at her even in the silence of her room:

Two Thousand People Believed Dead in Johnstown Flood

Her heart hammered in her chest. *Could Esther have been at Johnstown for the Memorial Day holiday?* Sleep impossible she slipped out of bed and picked up the newspaper once more. For days the disaster had been headline news, a stunned nation appalled and bewildered. Slowly, she raised the paper to catch the yellow pool of light from the lamp and began to read the article once more: *After a week of rain twenty million tons of water breached the dam and spillway of the North Fork Hunting and Fishing Club high in Pennsylvania's Allegheny Mountains sending a seventy-foot wave of water into the valley below, pulverizing the city of Johnstown. The devastation was unbelievable. More than four miles of debris lined the course of the Little Conemaugh River, including fifty miles of ruptured railroad track and thirty locomotives, and an estimated one hundred tons of barbed wire. Homes and stores were reduced to piles of stone, crushed brick, and shattered window glass.*

Amanda's stomach lurched as she read accounts of the dead—their bodies ripped of clothes, scalps torn from their heads and limbs severed. Some corpses were recovered as far as fifteen miles downstream, coming to rest on muddy hillsides amid the tangled limbs of trees.

But even if Esther and her family were at their cottage, would they have been physically effected? It sounded as though all of the damage was to the valley below the dam. Amanda had sent a telegram to Esther's home in Pittsburgh but received no reply. That did not bode well.

She read on: *Tomorrow, fifty undertakers from the State Capitol are scheduled to make their way by rail to the devastated site. On the same day a freight train will be dispatched from Pittsburgh carrying hastily constructed pine coffins.* Amanda squeezed her eyes shut to stay the tears as she imagined the piles of coffins, some of them miniaturized to accommodate the bodies of infants and small children. A vision of little Gail running along the shore of the sparkling little lake in the mountains shook her to the core.

The Valley Spirit ended with a plea for help. Volunteers were pouring in from all over the nation to help care for the survivors. Clara Barton and the Red Cross were erecting hospital tents, and Amanda's own Presbyterian Church of the Falling Spring in Chambersburg was organizing a group to travel to the stricken area next week. Therein lay the reason for her sleeplessness. Michael needed her help with reservations for the July opening. She already had train tickets and had promised to join him next week.

A group from her church was going to help the disaster victims. Amanda chewed on her lip, folded the newspaper and tossed it on the floor. She was being a ninny. Surely Esther and her family were safe. The breached dam was below their cottage. Aside from her need to know that her friend was all right there was nothing she could do to help those poor flood victims.

No!, her conscience shrieked. *Don't just throw the paper aside and the decision it demands. You can't throw compassion aside, as you can the newspaper, and go on with your com-*

fortable life. No!

Tomorrow she would contact the church. She would go to Johnstown. Michael would have to understand.

At the time of the great flood, Johnstown and its surrounding communities along the Conemaugh River at the confluence of Stoney Creek and the Little Conemaugh River were home to nearly thirty thousand residents. It was a blue-collar industrial town fifty miles from Pittsburgh, sitting in a deep valley between mountains with an ill-constructed earthen dam looming high above it. Citizens had been warned time and time again of danger if the dam broke but had grown complacent and ignored the first signs of real trouble. Now their town was no more.

The outpouring of the American people to the worst natural disaster ever to hit their country was unbelievable. Supplies poured in; volunteers to help with the aftermath of the flood came from as far away as California. Cincinnati sent twenty thousand pounds of ham, Arbuckle's in Pittsburgh thirty thousand pounds of coffee, a New York butcher one-hundred-fifty pounds of bologna, and prisoners of Western Penitentiary in Pittsburgh baked a thousand loaves of bread a day. Standard Oil Company shipped barrels of kerosene. A carload of potatoes came from Walla Walla, Washington. Lumber, furniture, embalming fluid, pitch, pine tar, and resin arrived daily. Money from all of the major cities poured into Johnstown along with nickels and dimes from school children and convicts.

Several days after the flood the relief train left Harrisburg with Amanda aboard and inched its way over flooded tracks and damaged bridges to Altoona. There the group from Chambersburg was forced to leave the train and travel the rest of the way by horse-drawn carriage.

The closer they drew to the devastated city the more heart-rending the scene became. The roads were lined with homeless people, some carrying only a framed picture or a solitary chair, the only thing saved from their homes, their faces a mask of hopeless misery. Busy workers were engaged in clearing away the piles of driftwood and scattered articles of household goods. Beds, bureaus, soaked and muddy mattresses, chairs, tables, pictures, highchairs, overcoats, shoes and remnants of clothing still littered the tracks and roads. At South Fork, men were transferring a pile of what Amanda guessed were at least a hundred corpses from a freight car to open wagons, a grueling task, indeed.

At last she reached Tony by telegraph and he replied: "In Johnstown. Esther missing."

Amanda and the volunteers from Chambersburg were directed to the First Presbyterian Church, a large brick edifice in the center of the city, one of Johnstown's few remaining buildings. She had gotten a message to Tony that she would meet him at the church. The minute she saw his ravaged face she suspected the worst.

She embraced him and they settled into an empty pew. "Tell me what happened. Why was Esther in Johnstown? Is she dead?"

"I don't know." Tony rubbed the black stubble on his cheeks. "She was with child . . . not due for another month . . . but on Wednesday she began having pains. We were worried. Because of the heavy rains the roads were a sea of mud and if she were to go into labor a midwife might not be able to get up the mountain. Johnstown has a lying-in hospital so I decided to take her there, just to be safe." He shook his head and began to sob. "Gad, what a mistake that was."

"Then what?" Amanda prompted.

"We had promised Gail she could see the Memorial Day parade the next day so after we got Esther settled at the hospital

I looked for overnight accommodations. The hotels were all full. There was a convention of The Ancient Order of Hibernians, but eventually I secured a room for one night. Memorial Day morning, Gail and I visited Esther and her pains had stopped. The doctor suggested we leave her one more day, then take her back to Pittsburgh. So when the parade was over, I took Gail home to pack. I planned to leave the next day." He jumped up and began to pace. "The next morning . . . Friday . . . it was dark, with billowing thunderclouds, and raining hard. Several men from neighboring cottages stopped by and asked me to go with them to inspect the lake. For several days prior to Memorial Day, storm after storm had swept across the mountains and flooded every creek and rivulet. The little South Fork which runs into the upper end of the lake was a raging torrent and the lake was higher than I'd ever seen it. At this point water had begun to pour over the top of the dam. The dam itself, wretchedly built of mud and boulders, was saturated and leaking copiously so Colonel Under, the president of the fishing club, sent twenty-five Italians to try to fix it. If the club members had only opened the fish screens when the lake began to rise it might have helped but the fools didn't want all of the freshly stocked fish to escape.

"Several men got across the dam and rode into town to raise a warning to the residents." Tony's cheeks glistened with tears. "The people had heard dire warnings about the lake for so many years it was like crying *wolf*. They ignored the alarm.

"I didn't want to risk taking Gail into town. I thought she would be safer here, so I took her to the clubhouse where several of the help and a few guests were staying. I asked them to watch her while I rode into town and brought Esther back to the cottage. I had a terrible premonition of disaster." Tony's face twisted in bitterness. "Ironically the millionaires were safer up there beside the monstrous lake they had created than down in the valley where the innocent lived and worked. Anyhow, I knew I couldn't get a carriage through the roads so I saddled

Esther's horse and put it on a lead. As I approached the dam, I heard a sound like a tremendous peal of thunder. Trees, rocks, and earth shot into the air in great columns as the dam gave way and a wall of water almost forty feet high, millions of tons of it, went crashing, roaring, and howling into the Conemaugh valley."

Again Tony broke down and Amanda put her arms around his heaving shoulders. When he could resume, he said, "I had to turn back. There were no roads, no way to get through. So I waited. And waited. In the end I could stand it no longer and I set out on foot. It took me an entire day to get down the mountain. You see what I found. The hospital was gone. God help us, the entire town was gone."

"There is no trace of Esther?"

Tony shook his head. "I have been searching for days. I've looked at every dead body recovered." He bit his lip. "I haven't given up, though, Amanda. There have been some miraculous rescues of individuals who were swept downstream and are being cared for in homes still standing."

"Is Gail still at the clubhouse?"

"No. Her grandparents were able to get through yesterday and they took her back to Pittsburgh."

"I'm here with a volunteer group from our church. I needn't stay with them. I want to join you in your search, Tony."

"There really isn't much you can do, except be on the lookout for people bringing survivors to the makeshift hospital being set up on the edge of town." He swallowed. "And, of course, check the dead as they are recovered from the rubble."

Amanda looked up and saw a tall, imposing, white-haired gentleman approaching them. The pastor of the church had gathered the volunteer group from Chambersburg in the front of the church and when he saw Tony and Amanda talking he came back to speak to them.

"Are you with the church group?" he asked.

"I am," Amanda said. "My friend here is searching for his wife who was in Johnstown at the time of the flood."

"And I must go," Tony said. "I understand several survivors have been brought in from Sandy Vale and are at the tent hospital. Amanda, I am staying at the clubhouse. I . . . I will locate you somewhere if I find her." He didn't give her a chance to reply but hurried up the aisle and out of the church.

"Terrible, terrible tragedy," the minister said. "It is a miracle our church is still standing. About one hundred and seventy-five people took refuge here during the flood. After a tremendous crash of water, when most of us expected to die, I began to pray fervently that the lives of those in the church might be spared." He puffed out his chest. "No second crash came and the water passed us by. I believe my prayers saved us; however, most of the pews were demolished. As you can see the ones that remain are being used to hold coffins. The cleaning and embalming take place on either side of the pulpit and then the bodies are placed in coffins and put across the ends of the pews near the aisles so that people can file past and identify them. These are nearly all bodies of our parishioners." He smiled at Amanda. "You can help here if you wish. The bereaved need help and solace dealing with the identification of a loved one." Amanda thought the pastor seemed more than a little smug about his role in the disaster. She would rather work with Tony to find Esther or volunteer at the hospital but she began to get some idea of what the week ahead might be like.

When she didn't respond, he walked her up the aisle to join her friends. "Part of your group might want to go to Kernsville, a settlement just south of town where the Red Cross has established its headquarters."

"I would like that," Amanda said. "I have been quite interested in nursing and social work. Maybe I could do some work that would help with search and rescue while I also look for my friend."

Several other women also indicated that they would like to go to Kernsville. They were given directions and a church member offered to lead them across town. As they filed out of the church they saw freight cars, both emptied and loaded, that had actually been lifted from the tracks by the rushing water, carried a distance of several blocks and deposited in the church graveyard where they were lying on top of tombstones and monuments.

The group crossed a slender footbridge two hundred feet above the waters of Stony Creek to a plateau where acres of white tents had been erected. "This is the camp of the American National Red Cross," their guide explained. "It is under the direction of its president, Miss Clara Barton, and is the first real test of Miss Barton's new organization."

Amanda was deeply impressed as they were led through the encampment. "Everything is exquisitely neat," she commented to the other ladies. "The boards of the tent floors are almost as white as the snowy linens on the cots. I think Miss Barton has done a fantastic job under the circumstances." Her glance swept the area and she took a deep breath. The contrast here to the horrible filth of the town, with its fearful stench and streets piled with dead animals, was a welcome relief.

The centerpiece of the camp was one large hospital tent capable of accommodating forty persons. Eight smaller tents, large enough for twenty persons each, clustered around it like chicks around a hen. Beyond the hospital and kitchen tents the group entered the Quartermaster's tent where a little flag snapped brightly in the breeze. They were greeted by Clara Barton.

Amanda looked at her in surprise. She had studied about the renowned Clara Barton in science class and had a mental picture of a tall, statuesque woman with a commanding presence. Instead the Clara Barton standing in front of her was a little woman in a plain black dress and muddy boots. She was several inches shorter than Amanda who was only five-foot, two inches.

Miss Barton's resolute voice, however, belied her small stature. "Thank you for coming, folks," she said. "We can certainly use volunteers. Where is your group from?"

"Chambersburg," one of the men answered.

"I know the town. General Lee assembled his forces there before his ill-fated encounter with the Union at Gettysburg." A shadow moved across Miss Barton's face. "It was a real disaster that we were not prepared for. Here, at Johnstown, we have an organized Red Cross with fifteen physicians and four trained nurses. At present we are conducting a house-to-house canvas to see how many people need attention. I would like volunteers for this mission. A large number of residents with serious injuries have been too weak or broken in spirit to seek help. You can assure the needy that help is available and then report back to us when and where a doctor or nurse is needed." She fixed them with her bright black eyes. "Be gentle. In addition to being battered and bruised you will find many citizens suffering temporary insanity from the life threatening fright they have had. Lavinia Dock, one of our nurses, will direct you."

Amanda's ears perked up at the mention of Lavinia Dock.

"I would like to volunteer to work with Miss Dock," Amanda said. "She lectured at my college."

"Good. The rest of you can help with the distribution of blankets, clothing, and food. Sleeping tents have been set up on the periphery for doctors and volunteers." She waved her hand toward a young girl standing nearby. "My assistant will show you the way. Meals are served in the mess tent. Get a good night's sleep and report back here tomorrow by eight o'clock."

Early the next morning Amanda reported to the hospital to walk the aisles of all of the tents in search of any new arrivals and look for Esther. She was just leaving the tent housing amputees when she saw a doctor bent over a cot. He looked vaguely familiar. She hesitated and then walked back inside to get a better look. When he straightened up and turned his head she gave a gasp of surprise. It was George.

He saw her immediately and came striding toward her. He grasped both of her hands in his and gave her a hug. "Tony told me you were here. I've had my eye out for you ever since I arrived. Have you heard the good news? He has found her and she is alive."

"Oh, thank God. Where? When? Is she injured?"

"Come outside with me. We can talk better there," he said.

Once outside the hospital tent he began to explain. "This is hard to believe but the house she was staying in was brick and it was lifted *intact* from its foundation by the surging flood. Amanda, the waters carried it more than two miles and deposited it in the Sandy Vale School playground. There were two women inside, Esther and a midwife. A local farm family found them and took them to their home. Esther had gone into labor. She gave birth the next day. A little girl."

"Is she here? Can I see her?"

"No. Esther had no identification and she was suffering from hysteria. Tony heard some women in the hospital tent talking about a woman who had given birth during the flood at Sandy Vale so he went to investigate. He found her there. He came back here to tell me and is out looking for a place where the telegraph lines are still intact so he can notify our parents. I understood him to say he would go straight back to Sandy Vale and return to Pittsburgh from there."

"Is she all right?"

George's face clouded. "Tony said she is very confused. She didn't seem to know him."

"Oh, dear."

"It's best that he's getting her back to Pittsburgh and a good hospital. He will keep in touch and I will go home as soon as I can leave here."

Amanda's gaze swept George's appearance. He was older, all trace of boyishness gone. His hair had begun to recede from his brow but it was still full and he wore glasses which he hurriedly removed and stuffed into the pocket of his white coat. "I should have guessed you would be here," she said with a slow smile.

"Yes. I came as soon as I got word of the disaster. And you?"

"The same. I am volunteering with a group from our church in Chambersburg." She lifted the pocket watch pinned to the waist of her skirt and looked at the time. "I must go. We are to get our assignments at eight o'clock."

"I must go, too. Doctors are needed desperately. Why don't we meet in the mess tent, tonight? I may know more then."

"Fine." With that Amanda scurried away to the Red Cross Headquarters tent where Lavinia was working. After introducing themselves they set out under cold, gray clouds hanging low above the hills to check the few homes in the town still standing. Johnstown was a noisy place. It rang with the shouts of men pulling at ropes and the crash of timbers and roofs as they pulled down wrecked buildings. Picks and shovels, chains and axes rang as they were directed upon heaps of debris. Foul smoke hung in the air where dead animals were being burned. Volunteers were poling light skiffs about the streets still covered with water to take passengers from place to place. Lavinia hailed one of the boats to traverse a particularly devastated area.

"It's rewarding to see the outpouring of help from the towns-people, many of whom I'm certain have lost everything they have," Amanda commented as they alighted from the skiff and lifted their skirts to wade through ankle-deep water.

"But not all men are responding to the crises in a humane manner," Lavinia told her. "Some are more like wild beasts than human beings. Bands of looters roam the streets and I hear stories about terrible acts of plunder. One man was caught cutting off a dead woman's finger to get at a costly ring."

Amanda nodded. "I've heard similar stories. Still, I see more acts of kindness than I do evil."

Lavinia smiled sweetly. "I guess that is why we are both here."

Twilight was falling when Amanda found George in the mess hall. He looked harried and gray with fatigue. "I can't stay," he said. "They are still bringing victims in by the dozen. I am needed in the surgical tent. Anyway, I don't know any more about Esther. Tony is with her."

"Then, go. I understand. I'll catch up with you tomorrow."

Early in the morning of Amanda's third day in Johnstown she reported to the Red Cross administration tent and was approached by a tall, stylish woman who looked to be in her fifties, with typical brunette coloring. The woman introduced herself as Lillian Wald.

"I understand you have experience working with children," Miss Wald said. "Would you be interested in helping with the Pennsylvania Children's Aid Society where they're caring for orphans of the flood?"

Amanda grinned with pleasure. "I would be glad to."

"We have a number of orphans," Miss Wald told her. "Not as many as you might think because, unfortunately, the helpless children drown first . . . not their parents. But many of the survivors are living with relatives or neighbors and have to be identified and placed. I know of one compassionate family who has cared for one-hundred-fifty-seven children since the flood, and we have reports that many more orphans are being sheltered in homes as far away as Milltown."

They set out together and walked the mile into town where the society had set up an office in a little cottage just above the waterline in the upper part of the city. Walking briskly Miss

Wald filled her in on the organization's background. "The Society is headquartered in Philadelphia but when they heard of the tragedy they dispatched two efficient women and in the short time since their arrival they have confiscated this cottage and identified and placed more than fifty children with relatives."

Amanda felt a rising tide of interest. She would love to work with the children.

She and Miss Wald worked all day in the little office processing requests. Offers for those likely to be in need of a home had been pouring in from all over the country.

"Look at this," Amanda said, handing a piece of paper to Miss Wald. "It's a telegram from an orphanage in New York offering to care for seventy-five orphans and I have a similar request from Pittsburgh. In fact there are dozen of offers from large cities . . . Indianapolis and Cleveland, even Los Angeles . . . and small towns like Altoona and Apollo, Pennsylvania."

Miss Wald frowned. "In our haste, we must be careful that these are legitimate, trustworthy people. I've noticed one strange thing happening all too often. Many offers are made by churches and restricted by curious provisions pertaining to the religious belief of the orphans."

"I don't understand."

"Well, for example, just yesterday I saw a request from a Philadelphia minister for children of the Baptist faith and another from a minister who volunteered to look after a few sound Episcopal waifs."

Amanda had a sudden unsettling vision of little Bobby Keefer. How sad it was that any child might be denied a loving home because of the nature of his birth—either physical or religious.

That evening, to ease their depression, she and several from their group exchanged light-hearted stories about some of the queer salvage taken from the flood.

Amanda grinned. "A cat was found alive today after being buried in debris for a week. Every speck of hair was singed off and one eye was gone, but it was able to purr in the arm of the man that picked it up. He named it "Lucky" and carried it off to keep as a relic of the flood."

A woman laughed. "I heard a white Wyandotte rooster and two hens were also dug out alive, from the center of a heap of wrecked buildings, with completely dry feathers. They strutted off, highly indignant."

Amanda chuckled. "That reminds me of Penelope, the pet chicken I had when I was little. She thought she was my baby and never did associate with the other chickens."

"Speaking of babies," another woman said, "did you hear about the baby that was found floating in its cradle eighty miles downstream. It had a birthmark on its forehead and when the relief station where it was taken reported the mark on its description of survivors, the baby's mother was able to claim it. The infant was completely unharmed."

And on and on it continued—one story of survival after another.

Late on Thursday Lavinia sought Amanda out and suggested they share a cup of coffee in the dining tent.

"Did you always want to be a nurse?" Amanda asked as they took a seat at one of the tables.

"Heavens no. When I entered the Bellevue Training School several years ago professional nursing still was not considered a field acceptable for *ladies*. But I am a rebel," she said with a twinkle in her eyes. "Nursing, until the mid 1800s, was in the hands of charitable religious orders or was carried out by un-trained women who worked in hospitals for no more than thirty-five cents an hour. The hospital in its early stage staffed the hospital wards with pauper nurses, some of whom were short-term prisoners. Nurses were regarded as little better than lower-class housemaids and no respectable woman would stoop to such work. The person to change all that was Florence Nightingale. What a woman! She captured the imagination of the public and changed the image of the nurse. She called for specialized education and training because she said nursing was an art and training was as necessary for that as for any other art. That line of thinking inspired me."

"Have you ever met her?"

"No. She resides in London. She wrote her regrets that she could not come to Johnstown to be of assistance but she is quite ill. I've adopted Clara Barton as my role model. I served with her during the yellow fever epidemic in Florida and got to know her quite well. Clara is quite an inspiration . . . dedicated to nursing and women's rights. She served during the Civil War, the Franco-Prussian War and for a time even ran a women's prison in Massachusetts. After establishing the American branch of the International Red Cross she worked in Ohio during the floods in '84 and in Texas during the '87 famine."

"Where do you go from here? You only came to help with the flood didn't you?"

"I plan to work with Lillian Wald, the nurse you have been helping, at a settlement house on New York's Lower East Side once she gets one established."

"My goodness. That is quite a calling."

Lavinia sighed. "I feel very fulfilled. It's my dream to enhance the image of nursing as a career for women. These are proving to be the happiest years of my life."

"Are you from New York, then?"

Lavinia smiled. "Actually, dear, I'm from Pennsylvania, not far from you. I grew up in Harrisburg and I am quite familiar with Chambersburg and your beautiful Wilson College. As you know, I've lectured there. My sister Mira is interested in botany and has been collecting the seeds of various kinds of pine trees from all over the world. She is looking to buy some land near your Mt. Alto forest area in order to grow seedlings."

"But other than Florence Nightingale what really directed you to nursing as a career? Given its dubious status as a profession it had to be more than that."

Lavinia pursed her lips. "Believe it or not I was a pianist, planning to enter the professional music field. But when I was seventeen, working with the great Polish violinist Adamowski, I heard him remark to my teacher in a most patronizing tone that I would make a *good wife*. Something in his tone inferred that was *all* I could do. I felt keen mortification and a sense of alarm. In a flash, I seemed to see my freedom gone, myself a household drudge, and no way out. I said to myself, *I never will, I never will be just a wife,* and that determination has stayed with me."

Amanda nodded her head. "I know what you mean. I had to fight my stepfather to go to college. He insisted that a woman's place was in the home, raising a family. My fiancé feels much the same. Most men seem to think we don't know anything else. They fancy the longer we are kept ignorant of political affairs the better for all parties concerned. I wanted . . . demanded really . . . an education. But still, a college girl's life is secluded; we were cut off from the outside world and compelled to find our enjoyment, as well as our work, among ourselves."

Lavinia smiled. "I know. My sisters and I were educated in private schools. Then, when I was twenty-four, I read an article in *The Century* that changed my life. The article, *A New Profession for Women*, depicted in powerful detail the grim plight of the sick in city tenements and the urgent need for nursing reform. The writer singled out the new Belleville Training School for Nurses in New York for its unprecedented reform of nursing practices. It lit a spark in me, Amanda. No profession is more in need of reform than nursing. Earlier in the century, many police courts routinely offered prostitutes the choice of sentences: prison or hospital work. In the 1870s, just a little more than fifteen years ago, investigators found nursing at Belleville still in the hands of female ex-convicts. Wards were filthy, care was primitive and drunkenness common."

"But things are changing now aren't they?" Amanda asked. "I have been so impressed with the organization and cleanliness of this Red Cross camp. You, Miss Wald, and Miss Barton have such full, exciting careers. I . . . I feel my life has been so empty of purpose."

"But I believe you told me you were working for the Children's Aid Society in Chambersburg. That's rewarding."

At that moment a doctor stuck his head in the dining room and motioned to Lavinia. "I know you have had a full day, but we have an emergency in the operation theater. Can you assist me?"

Lavinia jumped to her feet. "Of course, I'll be right there." She turned to Amanda. "I know you leave soon. I'll be glad to write to you if you have any further questions. Get my address from Miss Barton. And thank you for your help."

Now that Amanda knew Esther was safe she was anxious to return to Chambersburg and prepare to join Michael on St. Simons. After breakfast she wandered outside looking for George. She found him striding across the hospital grounds, coffee in hand, dressed in street clothes.

"I was on my way to find you," he said. "Miss Barton said you were leaving tomorrow."

"We catch a train for Harrisburg at ten. Have you had any word about Esther?"

"Only that they are home and Esther is in the hospital." He frowned. "We haven't had much time to talk. I'm free today, if you can get away. It's a beautiful day . . . how about a hike?"

Amanda glanced in disbelief at the ravaged mountains around

them.

"Not here," he said quickly. "The hills to the east are greening up and quite beautiful. And the view from Kinley Peak is breathtaking. Esther and I loved to climb it when we were kids."

"I don't know," she said slowly. "How would we get there?"

"Horseback. Do you have a riding skirt?"

"Yes."

George grinned. "Then go tell Miss Barton that you have an assignment with Dr. Carbaugh and let's go. You need a break from all this foul air and misery."

By midmorning they were on their way. At the base of the mountain they tethered their horses to hike the rest of the way. A trail led through a stand of hemlocks into a deeper stand of oaks and maples. George walked ahead pulling branches out of her way and helping Amanda over the occasional fallen tree.

As they walked, their conversation was intermittent—their attention focused on the indistinct trail. Squirrels skittered up tree trunks and birds zipped from branch to branch. The air smelled of honeysuckle, sassafras and leaf mold. As the slope steepened Amanda's breathing became labored and conversation halted altogether. George led with a long stride and it was hard to keep pace. Her boots felt heavy as a bucket of sand and a blister was definitely in the picture. She was sweating profusely and began to wonder if there was any way she could save face and still ask: *How much further?* But then the grade became more gradual. In no time they were on a rocky peak exposed to the open sky and the breathtaking view George had promised.

Far below them a river snaked through a valley of orderly farm land. A tiny village, looking like the set under a Christmas tree, sparkled in the sunlight. "Now," George said, "wasn't the climb worth it?"

"It certainly was." She pointed to a flat spot on one of the rocks. "Can we sit down to enjoy it?"

George laughed. He brushed dirt from the rock and lent her a hand while Amanda gathered her long skirt and settled down. As she began to gingerly remove her boot, he opened the knapsack slung over his shoulder, pulling out sandwiches and a canteen.

Then he sat down a few feet away—a gentleman's distance.

While they ate, he reminisced about the summers his family had spent at South Fork. He and a buddy had often hiked the mountain trails around the lake, outfitted with tent and coonskin caps, pretending to be Daniel Boone. He described in detail the largemouth bass he caught one summer that still held the record for the lake. Amanda told a few fish tales of her own, about learning to use a fly-rod to catch wily native brown trout in the even-temperature of Falling Spring creek. Conversation with George was easy and carefree—not tense and urgent as conversations with Michael were wont to be.

All of a sudden Amanda began to scratch. "Ei, ei, ei," she muttered. "Your mountain has mosquitos."

George looked at her quizzically. "Ei, ei, ei? Where does that come from?"

"My mother was German and her mother spoke German in our home." She laughed. "It crops up once in a while in my speech."

"My mother is third generation German but I never heard it spoken. And your father? Was he German too?"

Amanda sighed. There it was again—the hated reminder of her illegitimacy. She could never admit her dark secret to this well-bred doctor. *What would he think of her?*

"I'm not sure," she said softly.

The sunlight began to wane and George suggested they start back down the mountain. He drew near as he helped her to her feet and for a second Amanda felt a flood of warmth flush her cheeks. *This would never do.*

She was tired and the blister on her heel throbbed so when

they got back to the hospital grounds she said she wanted to go directly to her tent. George looked disappointed but agreed. They paused before the flap of her tent.

He looked deep into her eyes. "If it wasn't for Michael. . . ." His voice trailed off.

"I know."

Then they parted—she went into her tent, he went down the hill to his.

The next morning, impatient to be home, Amanda boarded the train with her church group for the return trip to Chambersburg. She needed to sit by the tranquil Falling Spring creek and breathe country air free of the stench of death and the stink of burning pine tar, to replace the screeching of saw and thud of a hammer with the more serene warble of wrens and whistle of bobwhites. As the train entered the lush Cumberland valley the steep inclines of the Pennsylvania mountains leveled off to open, rolling fields. Split-rail fences marked the boundaries of well-tended farms. Honeysuckle bloomed by the roadside; wild roses climbed low stone pasture fences; pastures were dotted with cows and colts pranced beside their mares. Spring leaves were still tender and green. Startled rabbits ran from the sound of the train whistle as it hung in the warm air.

However, pretty as the rolling scenery was, Amanda's thoughts were confused and uneasy. The echo of Lavinia Dock's words *I never will . . . I never will be just a wife* preyed on her mind.

Clara Barton, Lillian Wald, Lavinia Dock—vital women with purpose in their lives. Women who would leave their mark.

She tapped her fingers on the train's windowsill. She remembered the look of gratitude on the face of an elderly woman when Amanda made a simple sling for her injured arm, remembered the young woman carrying an empty highchair through the streets searching for her baby, remembered the bewildered look of homeless children. Her life journey, which, as a college girl, had seemed so uncomplicated, presented choices she had never contemplated.

Chapter Ten

Soon after arriving home Amanda received one brief note from Tony saying that Esther was under psychiatric care at St. Francis Hospital in Pittsburgh. She was showing signs of improvement and he hoped to have her home soon. The baby was healthy and gaining weight. They had named her Ruth.

Now she sat in her room reading and rereading the letter from Michael that had come while she was in Johnstown, trying to find some degree of comfort in it. But there was none—he was plainly angry. He did not understand her need to delay her plans to help with the opening of the hotel. He had hired an *attractive* local girl to work in the office and later serve as hostess. She noticed his use of the word *attractive*. Was that a warning? Was this the same attractive girl who'd helped Michael with the decorating? Unrest cast a dark shadow over her. Still, he wrote that he missed her and wanted to get married as soon as possible. He did not understand the delay.

Nor did she. She did not know what had changed her. Perhaps it was that she had crossed the great Rubicon that had always separated girls from women. She had wanted to know what love was, what the girls in college giggled about. She had done the Dirty Deed. But since her night of passion with Michael, she had grown reflective as she tried to picture her future with him. After all she was a woman now, not a naive child. They were no longer playmates—they were lovers. Lovers? That hardly seemed the word. It had been only one night, one evening. She had returned to her room, slept in her own bed, then woken the next morning to say good-bye to him once more. Since then, sex had not been spoken of in letters but it had been there between the lines. Absence had not lessened what she felt for him, she thought of him every day. Yet, something had changed. A boundary had been crossed. But if she was no longer an innocent child neither was she unworldly enough to believe that love alone would sustain a long distance romance indefinitely. She needed to go to St. Simons if she did not want to lose Michael.

Amanda's chin quivered with resolve. Silvia had graduated from college and Amanda had engaged no new tutoring students for the fall term. Tomorrow she would tender her resignation to the Children's Aid Society and make train reservations to the island. She spent a restless night during which she dreamed that she was lost in the teaming New York tenements. She woke in a panic—her nightgown soaked with sweat. Unable to go back to sleep she got up, lit an oil lamp and tried to read, but she could not concentrate. Exasperated, she slammed the book shut and made herself a cup of tea.

At long last the sky began to lighten, birds began to sing, and the interminable night was over.

Later that morning, resignation letter in hand, Amanda rolled her new bicycle out of the little carriage house. The bicycle, a birthday gift from her mother and step-father, was new on the market— bright red with tires of equal height— to accommodate the long, full skirts of. She was certainly glad to be rid of her old bicycle with its impossibly high front wheel from which she had taken many a spill.

She was humming as she peddled into town, in better spirits now that her decision was made, pausing on the Market Street bridge to admire the lovely waterfall where Falling Spring Creek joined the Conococheague. It was one of those exceptionally clear June days with the sun high, puffs of clouds drifting through an azure sky, showy catalpa trees bending low with white blossoms. Amanda turned right off Market onto North

Franklin Street. The going was steeper now and she bit her lip as she peddled up Federal Hill. She slowed and turned onto Miller Street where the Children's Aid perched on the corner. A rain squall had come and gone during the night and the streets were wet, puddled and slippery. The air smelled fresh, welcome after the stink of Johnstown, and Amanda quivered with pleasure to be home again.

She turned in at the Children's Aid and parked her bicycle beside the front porch. She was hardly in the house when the door to the boy's room flew open. Bobby came hurtling down the hall and buried his face in her skirts as she wrapped her arms around him.

"I missed you," he cried. "Don't you never go 'way again."

Amanda felt her heart beating in her throat as she looked down at his homely little face streaked with tears. Mucus ran from his nose and he swiped it with his sleeve. She had let this child become way too fond of her and had given him no consideration in formulating her plans to leave Chambersburg. Bobby Keefer had never known love—he had only known pain and rejection—and that was a terrible thing. Dare she do the same to him?

She leaned down and kissed the top of his head. "I missed you too, young fellow. But I had to go help some poor children who need new homes. Have you been good for the matron?"

He nodded his head, then began to sob in earnest. "Some son-of-a-bitch stole my truck."

"I'm sorry to hear that . . . now what have I told you about swearing?"

Bobby's lower lip quivered. "I think it was that scabby new boy what took it. Name's Jimmy. He looks shitty."

Amanda sighed. She was beginning to think changing Bobby's speech pattern was hopeless.

"It's a beautiful day . . . you should be out playing with the other children. Why don't we go out to the play-yard and I'll push you on the swing?"

The tears ended, he took her hand and looked up at her with adoring eyes.

Oh, dear!

That afternoon the matron came into the office wearing a worried frown. Her brown hair was tucked into a cap and she wore a pristine white apron covering a homespun dress. "Miss Kennedy," she said, "I'm afraid we have a problem with the Keefer boy. The little rascal has taken to picking fights. Several days ago he laid into a younger boy and hurt him pretty bad. Did he tell you about it?"

"He only told me that someone stole his truck."

"Hmm. Well, the fight might have been tit for tat, but Amanda, we can't hold a loose rein on that type of behavior. I'm talking to you about it because you and Bobby seem to have a bond of some sort."

"I'm afraid I have encouraged that."

"Is it because of his harelip?"

Amanda hesitated. "Partly, I guess. He will probably be institutionalized until he reaches maturity. No one should grow up without knowing love."

"I try to show affection to all the children, much as I can. We can only do so much here."

"I know, and you do a fine job. I'm not finding fault. I've been thinking that Michael and I might adopt him once we are married."

The matron's eyebrows drew together in a straight line. "Oh, I don't know as how that's a good idea at all. How does your fiancé feel about it?"

Amanda had to admit to herself that this was the first time she had given voice to the idea that had been festering in her subconscious for some time. Adopt Bobby? She was simply putting into words a possible conclusion to the problem of abandoning the child when she moved on with her life. "I haven't asked Michael, yet," she said quietly.

The frown deepened and the matron made a great business of straightening her apron. "I happen to know a bit about Bobby's kin. The Keefers are poor white trash from out near Red Bridge. Bobby's father was killed in a barroom brawl and his ma took to selling herself and refused to care for the boy. I know you are well intentioned and think you can transform Bobby, but I believe a child is born with his or her own character. Over time you could probably improve him. But change? Turn an aggressive, belligerent child into a dignified, self-controlled adult. Uh-uh. I don't think so."

Like the question posed in The Prince and the Pauper, Amanda thought. *Nature or nurture.*

"Don't you want children of your own, Amanda?" the matron asked.

"Of course, I want children."

"Well, I would give adoption a lot of thought if I were you." She smiled. "Such an undertaking would be very noble of you, but I question how wise it would be."

It has nothing to do with being noble, Amanda thought. *I made a mistake in letting him become too attached to me and now I feel guilty leaving him.* "I'm just thinking of his future and what yet another rejection might do to him," she said instead.

"Just be careful, my dear. Turning that boy around would be a mighty big undertaking. You have a wedding coming up and Mr. Orr tells me you have an interest in more schooling."

"I do, and thank you for your advice. I will talk to Bobby about fighting."

The matron left and Amanda closed her eyes. She had a sudden vision of Bobby reaching both of his arms out to her as though she belonged to him and him alone. Oh my, what a well-intentioned mess she had made of things.

• • •

The matron had no sooner gone than Mr. Orr stuck his head in the office.

"Welcome back, Amanda. Can I come in for a few minutes?"

"Of course."

After exchanging a few pleasantries he talked to her about writing an article for the paper about the situation in Johnstown. She filled him in on the monumental volunteer effort to clear away the rubble and mentioned the need to place additional orphans in facilities such as theirs.

"As you know, Miss Kennedy, we are almost full but I will talk to the board. Perhaps we can make room for one or two."

"That would be wonderful." Amanda took a deep breath and fingered the letter of resignation in her pocket. Should she? It would change the course of her life. But when she accepted Michael's ring she had made a commitment she could not bring herself to break.

She handed the letter to Mr. Orr.

"He unfolded the single sheet of stationery, then shook his head and gave it a cursory glance. "I have been afraid of this. Of course, we knew you planned a trip to Georgia to help with the opening of the hotel, but I thought you would return . . . that your wedding plans were still sometime in the future."

"I'm not certain what I will do when I get to St. Simons. Michael and I have been waiting for over eight years. If we want to have a family we can't wait much longer."

"I assume, then that you no longer plan to continue your education with an eye to nursing and a future in social work."

Amanda hesitated, then nodded her head. "At least for now."

Mr. Orr removed his spectacles and pinched his nose. He looked at her intently. "I sense some uncertainty in your words. I hate to see you go. You have been a real asset to us. Why don't I just I hold this letter until you are more positive of your future."

Amanda swallowed a lump in her throat. "Thank you, Sir.

The next day, Saturday, Amanda secured train tickets for Georgia and peddled her bicycle over to Coldbrook to say good-bye to her mother and siblings.

Sarah was in the parlor, knitting basket by her side, needles clicking. Amanda kissed her on her cheek and took a chair by her side.

"You seem to be knitting every time I see you, Mother. What is it this time?"

"A vest for Johnnie. I swear that boy grows inches overnight."

"Mom, I've come to say good-bye. I'm going down to St. Simons to help Michael with the grand opening."

The knitting needles continued to click. "Are you coming back or are you planning to stay?"

"I don't honestly know."

"Don't play with that boy's affection, Amanda. He deserves better."

"I know that. I plan to talk things out and make a decision one way or another." She sighed. "It isn't easy, Mother."

"Well, it should be. Either you love him or you don't. And don't give me any of that sass about wanting a career. Marriage to a fine man like Michael McKenzie should be enough career for any girl."

Amanda jumped to her feet. There was just no use trying to explain her unrest to her mother. "I'll write," she said, "when I know what I am going to do."

Sarah lowered her knitting to her lap. "You know I only want you to be happy, honey."

"I know. Where are the kids?"

"Johnnie is riding his new bicycle, but Eliza and Erin are in the back garden helping Ila plant beans."

"I'll stop and say good-bye to them, then I must get home. I have a lot of packing to do."

Back in her room she began to gather the dresses she would need for at least a two-week stay in Georgia. She did not bother to write Michael that she was coming—she would be there before any mail could reach him. If she decided to remain longer her mother could ship the rest of her belongings.

She worked slowly, rejecting first one garment, then another. She had never felt so unsettled. Somewhere in the room a fly buzzed, flailing against the window-pane. Amanda walked over and leaned her forehead on the cool glass of the window, staring blindly.

There was a tap at her door. "Miss Kennedy there is a gentleman in the parlor wanting to see you. I have his card."

Amanda opened the door and took the elegantly engraved card from the housekeeper. *Dr. George Carbaugh.*

She gave a delighted laugh. "Tell him I will be right down."

Amanda flew to the mirror and patted her hair into place, dusted her nose with powder, pinched her cheeks to give them color, and dabbed some toilet water behind her ears. Her shirt-waist dress was not one she would have chosen but it would simply take too long to change outfits. With a pert wiggle she straightened her skirt, hurried out the door and swept down the open staircase.

She found George in the parlor, arm tucked behind his back, admiring the view from one of the tall, deep-set windows flung wide open to catch all the scents and sounds of spring. Amanda swished across the room, surprised at the pleasure she felt in seeing him.

He took her hand and raised it to his lips, his somber gaze never leaving her face. Sudden fear pushed her joy aside.

"Esther!" she cried. "Is she worse?"

"No, she is improving every day. Tuesday, for the first time, she asked to nurse the baby. I am on my way back to Boston and thought I would stop to see you and bring you a first-hand report."

"I'm glad you did. How ever did you find me?"

"I engaged a carriage at the train station and they directed me here." He smiled. "The train master seemed to know exactly who I was asking about and, by the look on his face, he was very curious."

"My mother worked in the office."

"So, they said."

"I'm such a ninny to keep you standing here. Come, sit down and tell me all about Esther." They settled themselves on a medallion-back sofa and she rang the bell-pull to summon tea and scones. As they waited Amanda listened intently as George described Esther's treatments at the hospital and her steady recovery.

"How long can you stay," she asked, nibbling on a delicious cranberry scone.

"Until Monday morning. There is a six a.m. train to Philadelphia where I can connect to New York and then Boston. I'm anxious to get back to work."

For some unknown reason she did not tell George that she was also planning to leave—headed south to possibly stay and marry—while he was traveling north to pursue an exciting new career in medicine.

George's gaze strayed to the open window where the curtains were rustling in a gentle breeze. "I like Chambersburg. It's quite different from the steep hills and industrialization of western Pennsylvania. My life has been spent in large cities . . . Pittsburgh, Paris, and now Boston. I have only been to Chambersburg twice, once to escort Esther to the dance where I met you and then again to her graduation. Both stays were quite brief. I had the impression you lived with your family."

"I moved here after my mother remarried. I thought it time to strike out on my own."

George smiled. "Sounds like you." He pulled out his pocket watch and looked at the time. "I must secure lodging for tonight. The last time I was in Chambersburg I stayed at the Washington House. It was quite nice. I assume it's still here." He cocked his head. "I hope you are free to spend some time with me?"

Amanda's mind raced. It was terribly inconvenient, with all the packing she had to do, but she did want to spend time with him. She gave him a pert smile. "I would love to show you our pretty little town. Why don't I ride into town with you while you engage your room."

"That sounds like a novel idea. As I remember the Washington House has an excellent restaurant. We can have dinner there. Do you have a theater we could attend this evening?"

"As a matter of fact we do. The Rosedale Opera House is featuring a play by Thomas Hardy, or we can attend a live concert in the Diamond. The brass band from the village of St. Thomas is performing."

"Excellent. I'll let you choose." He started to rise.

"Let me get you another cup of tea while I change."

"No more tea, please. I see you have a great porch shaded by a huge oak tree. I'll wait for you there."

Under Amanda's tutelage George turned the carriage south on Main Street then west on Market Street. As they approached the hotel Amanda had a sudden inspiration. "Before we go into the Washington House to engage a room I want you to see Chambersburg's newest attraction. You may decide to stay there." She directed George to backtrack to Commerce Street where they drove past the Wolf Ball Park and Athletic Field then over the railroad tracks to the Wolf Company's mill and lake.

Amanda continued her commentary. "Five years ago Augustus

Wolf, an experienced millwright, came to Chambersburg to establish a partnership with Mr. Hamaker. He soon bought Mr. Hamaker's part of the business and the Wolf Company is fast becoming recognized as one of the finest milling companies in the country. Mr. Wolf is an avid fisherman and has a very deep interest in the Conococheague Creek which flows adjacent to the mill. Recently he decided to build a dam and impound the Conococheague that supplies water to his various shops. Wolf Lake & Park has grown into quite a complex with a swimming area, a bath house, a bowling alley, shuffleboard, carousel hors-es, and a boat house where canoes and row boats can be rented. But best of all there is a dance hall known as Dreamland and a one hundred foot tower with ten rooms and a restaurant for traveling visitors." She touched his arm. "Turn in here."

Being Saturday, the park was teeming with visitors and vendors selling post cards, candy dishes, pins and pennants. Screaming children, barking dogs and music from the carousel filled the air. George bought snow cones and they walked around the sparkling lake. "I would like to bring you here tomorrow and rent a boat if the weather permits," he said, "but I think I prefer to stay overnight at the Washington House. It is a little more sedate and I know they have a fine restaurant."

Amanda felt heat rise in her cheeks. He was a doctor. She should have known he was used to more tasteful accommodations. "I agree," she said. "We will simply retrace our steps and secure your room." She hesitated. "I would like to show you the Children's Aid where I work. It is on our way. Do you mind?"

"Of course not. Your choice of employment intrigues me."

Several small children were out in the play-yard under the watchful eye of the matron as Amanda and George approached the home. Bobby spotted Amanda immediately and came racing toward her. He skidded to an abrupt halt and grabbed her hand.

"Miz Manda, Miz Manda, I's got new boots," he said breathlessly, pointing to elaborately tooled cowboy boots. "Ain't they somethin'."

Amanda threw back her head and laughed. "Indeed they are. Where did you get such a fine pair?"

"Mr. Orr brung them. He says I gotta stop fightin' though or he gonna take them back." Bobby sobered as he became aware of the tall man standing at her side. He squinted as he looked up, his brow creased into deep furrows. "Who's that. What's he doin' here?"

"This is George Carbaugh. He is a doctor friend of mine from Pittsburgh."

"You sick?"

"No. Now, never mind . . . the matron is motioning for you to come back. I see the boys are playing mumbly-peg."

George had been looking intently at Bobby. "I have been considering a speciality in reconstructive surgery," he said to Amanda. "Do you think the boy would allow me to examine his lip?"

Bobby jumped back and hid behind Amanda's skirt. "No damn doctor gonna stick his finger in my mouth," he yelled.

Amanda pulled him forward and gave him a reassuring hug. "He won't hurt you, Bobby. He's a fine doctor. He might be able to fix the crease in your lip. You would like that, wouldn't you?"

"Yeah." He gave George a withering look. "Miz Manda's my friend. I guess if she says it's all right you can look at it."

George hunkered down and ran his fingers lightly over the damaged lip, lifting it carefully to examine the underside. "Hum," he said.

"Can you fix it?" Bobby said.

"No, not at this time. I only. . . ."

With a sob Bobby jerked himself free of Amanda's hand and ran back to the yard.

George looked stricken. "I'm sorry. I didn't mean to upset the child."

"Nor, did I. Bobby is an enigma. Tough as nails on the outside but a very sensitive little boy on the inside. What do you think, though? Is there an operation to repair that type of deformity?"

"New techniques are being developed all of the time. I would have to study more about cleft palate."

"I thought your speciality was Anatomy."

"It was but I am thinking of switching to Reconstructive Surgery. It is much more lucrative."

And George is used to a high standard of living, Amanda thought. But she didn't give voice to her thoughts. Instead she said, "Follow me. I'll give you a quick tour of the home." When they were finished she led him into her tiny office, slid into a chair behind her tidy desk. She smiled. "I confess this place has become like home to me."

He took one of the two guest chairs. "I can tell. It fits you, Amanda. You relate to these children." He pulled at his cuffs. "I assume that child with the harelip is an orphan."

"Yes. It's a terribly sad case. He was raised in the county jail and has known nothing but institutional care. The other children taunt him and with a deformity he is probably unadoptable. I'm afraid he has little chance for a normal life."

"Interesting," George said. "I would like to look closer at the lip after I study more about the cleft palate. Although it is quite disfiguring, it looked as though it might respond well to corrective surgery."

"But that would be terribly expensive. We have no funds for that type of thing. The society operates entirely on public donations and they are barely adequate to keep the doors open."

"Still, I would like to take another look at the boy. You have heard of attorneys doing a certain amount of charitable work. It is called *pro-bono*. Well, doctors do the same. It might be an interesting opportunity for me to hone my surgical skills." He grinned. "And it might give me an excuse to return to Chambersburg."

Amanda blushed and hastily rose. "We can stop and talk to Bobby on our way out. I'll explain to him that as a doctor you would like to come back and examine his lip further. I can't promise you he will cooperate."

"I'm good with children and I happen to have a sour ball in my pocket." He winked. "I'm very good at enticement."

Enticement? Amanda felt a rush of heat to her face. *What in the world was she getting herself into?*

They had an early dinner at the Washington House, then strolled uptown for a short walk before going to the theater. Over twenty years of hard work had brought Chambersburg out of the ashes of the Confederate firing in 1864 to a lovely, vibrant community. Trees graced the curbs and colorful awnings protected the wares displayed in front of Victorian facades. As they walked George commented on the ornate millwork around the roofs and windows of the new buildings.

"Chambersburg seems to have a vibrant economy for such a small town."

"We do. Industry of the post-war period has brought the Wolf Company, which you've seen, flour mills, a planing mill and a door factory. Henry Sierer and Company is said to be the largest furniture manufacturer in the Middle States. In addition we have T.B. Woods, maker of power transmission appliances, and the Chambersburg Engineering Company. Our growing economy is due in part to the expansion of rail service. The Cumberland Valley Railroad is a major hub of rail transportation on the east-west corridor. We are larger and more diverse than before the Confederates burned the town."

"I see they are installing electric streetlights."

"They are, and they say homes will have electric lights by the

end of this decade. Can you imagine that. And there is a tele-
phone line now between Waynesboro and Hagerstown just
twenty miles south of us. Chambersburg is interested in phone
service but there is some kind of conflict with the Bell Company. I'm sure they will get it resolved."

"Do you have a high school and hospital?"

"Not yet. We have the Chambersburg Academy, a large
preparatory school on the corner of East Queen and Third Street
close to the Washington Hotel where you are staying, and the
Children's Aid Society is very interested in founding a hospital."

"Tell me about this fire you mentioned."

"In 1864, before the end of the war, Confederate General
McCausland entered Chambersburg and demanded one hundred
thousand dollars in gold or five hundred thousand dollars in U.S.
currency. When the residents couldn't pay the ransom, McCausland ordered the destruction of the town. Over five hundred
homes and businesses were burned leaving over two thousand
people homeless."

"Goodness."

They walked around the Diamond and then north on Main
Street. "And here we are," Amanda said. "The Rosedale Opera
House. It was built on the site of the Rosedale Seminary, a girl's
school destroyed in the 1864 fire."

"It's much bigger than I expected."

Amanda grinned proudly. "It seats a thousand patrons for
both afternoon and evening entertainment. Quite an establishment for a little country town, don't you think?"

Sunday was sunny and warm, the hay-scented air cooled by an
earlier shower. Amanda dressed in one of the new, shorter,
"outing" dresses, her ankles self-consciously displayed. George
had on a pair of stiff, new Levi's with brass rivets and wore a
straw hat. He placed her picnic basket, together with a jug of

lemonade, in the back of the carriage and they set off.

George drove directly to the Boat House at Wolf Lake, the park already teeming with weekenders, children with dripping ice cream cones, couples arm in arm. Brightly painted boats rocked at anchor and a white sail sped by the dock in a dazzle of sunshine. Birds swooped overhead and everywhere there was activity and a great stir. George looked delighted.

A sign posted beside an open service counter told of "nearly fifty boats, including naphtha launches each headed by a 'captain.'" The sign also listed "many row boats for fishermen and canoes for the romantics."

A smile quirked the corner of George's mouth. "I really don't want a smelly gasoline engine and talkative captain and I certainly don't want to fish. I guess we must take the canoe."

"Are you familiar with canoes?"

"I come from Pittsburgh, dear. Home of the Allegheny, the Monongahela and Ohio Rivers. I've been boating since I was a child. And you?"

"We used canoes on the Conococheague behind the college all of the time."

"Then let's go." He walked over to the wooden ticket office and shook a clapper bell for service. A glass window flew up.

"Yes?"

"A two passenger canoe for the afternoon, please." George paid for the ticket and received a key to the padlock for canoe #24. "Are there any picnic facilities along the shore?" he asked.

"You could pull up on Round Island. You can't miss it. It's connected to both sides of the lake by a fancy bridge." The attendant directed a stream of tobacco juice to a hidden spittoon. "Pretty small though and gets crowded. Plenty of spots along the shore to picnic." He glanced at Amanda and added with a smirk, "That is if you want some privacy."

• • •

#24 was a handsome, bright-green canoe, freshly painted with yellow paddles. George put the picnic basket aboard and directed Amanda to a seat in the stern. He followed her into the canoe, picked up a paddle, and pushed off.

In the distance other boats dotted the lake filled with gayly dressed boys and girls in canoes or clumsy row-boats. Occasionally one could hear laughter or bits of their conversation. The glassy iridescent surface of the lake gleamed like molten glass, the shore lined with cattails and water lilies, great oaks, ash, and low-hanging willow trees. Beyond them loomed the humped backs of the dark and distant mountains. Amanda turned her face up to the sun, breathing deeply. The lightness, freshness and intoxication of the gentle air scarcely rippled the surface of the water. The bright sun, the quiet water, the lock-lock of the paddle as George rowed were hypnotic and for the first time in weeks Amanda felt completely at peace. She put her hand over the side of the canoe and trailed it in the clear water. George's hat was off, and the sight of his reddish-brown hair blown by the wind, the pale blue shirt he wore open at the neck with sleeves rolled back from tan forearms, and the yellow paddle held by him above the handsome green canoe, brought a flush to her face.

He followed the east bank of the lake and about a mile and a half from the boathouse rounded a point of land studded with a clump of trees and bushes covering a slank where there were scores of water lilies afloat, their huge leaves resting flat upon the still water.

"This looks like a good place to picnic," he said. "We can pull ashore and eat before taking a turn around the lake."

"Good. I don't know about you but this sun has made me hungry and I'm afraid my chunk of river ice in the hamper has melted by now."

George maneuvered the canoe next to a small honey-colored beach and seized the root of a willow to hold the boat still.

"Step square in the center, that will balance the boat, then step out carefully," he instructed.

Bossy, Amanda thought.

She reached up and grabbed an overhanging willow branch to steady herself. As she stepped out, her toe caught the handle of the picnic basket. She let go of the branch and lost her balance as the canoe careened to one side. With a cry she lurched over the side into the shallow water.

George reacted immediately and using the paddle to stabilize the canoe stepped into the water beside her. The water was only a few inches deep but Amanda was drenched. She lay there stunned with humiliation. Then she started to laugh. What a ninny!

George put his hands under her arms and raised her to her feet.

"Are you hurt?" he asked.

"No . . . only my pride." Her hair had come loose of its pins and lake water trickled down her face. His arms were still around her, his dark eyes locked on hers, his breath hot on her cheek. He lifted a hand to push her hair back from her face and then, as though it were the most natural thing in the world, he lowered his lips to hers.

For a brief moment she responded to his kiss, then gently pulled away. She began to tremble—either from the shock of her fall, her wet clothes or her reaction to his kiss.

George noticed and with one arm around her waist led her ashore to a sunny spot on the tiny beach. He retrieved the picnic basket from the boat and spread a faded tablecloth on the ground for her to sit. "I'll build a small fire to dry you off," he said. He began to round up several rocks which he arranged in a ring, took matches and the paper receipt for the canoe, some chips of driftwood and brush and kindled a fire. While Amanda settled herself on the tablecloth and began to unload the picnic basket he found more wood and soon had a nice fire going.

While they shared their lunch Amanda found herself babbling about trivia—never looking into George's eyes. He eventually reached over and took her hand. "We can't ignore what just happened," he said softly. "I think you know how I feel."

"But, I'm engaged, George." She lowered her head. "I'm so confused. Things once seemed so simple. Now, I don't know where my life is headed. I have a choice. I can go to Georgia and marry Michael as everyone expects. Or I can do the unthinkable and choose a career over marriage and enter nursing school."

"First of all, you should never marry because of other's expectations. Do you love Michael?"

Amanda twisted the ring on her finger and swallowed. "That's what is so hard. I no longer know what true love really is. I think I love him . . . he has been the center of my dreams since I was a child. But as we matured I began to see the differences in what we want from life and I question them. Michael has a picture in his mind of the woman he wants as a wife. Someone subservient to him. Someone to keep a neat home, bear him children, and act as a charming Southern hostess when the occasion demands. I want more than that."

"Things will happen the way they're meant to," George said. "You are a stoic. I believe there's a design and a form to everything. Nothing happens without a reason. Fate led us to meet again at Johnstown. When we shared that hike up the mountain I felt a strong physical attraction to you. I believe you felt the same for me."

Amanda forced a smile. "George, if I have learned one thing it is that physical attraction isn't enough to build one's life around." She jumped to her feet and shook the sand from her skirt. "I"m dry now and we are wasting a beautiful day."

Dusk was coloring the sky a deep purple when Amanda and George arrived back at her lodging. He jumped down from the carriage seat and walked around to hand her down, then held her elbow until they reached the front door. He was quiet, yet obviously miffed at something.

"Would you care to come in?" she asked shyly. "I can't take you up to my room but I am allowed to use the kitchen. I could make some coffee."

"A drink maybe. Have you any brandy or whiskey?"

She shook her head no. "I'm sorry. Mrs. Morrow doesn't allow hard liquor. We have some wine though."

"It doesn't matter. I really should be going. I've an early morning train."

When he made no effort to kiss her good-bye Amanda felt a strange tug at her heart. Surprisingly, she experienced a sickening feeling of disappointment.

"It's been a lovely day. I enjoyed it," she said summoning a smile. "Even falling in the water."

"I enjoyed it too." He gave her an arch smile. "Especially lifting you out of the water."

Amanda laughed and felt her face flush with red.

George tipped his hat, walked back to the carriage, and hopped onto the seat. With a vague wave of his hand he drove into the darkening evening.

The next morning Amanda dressed for travel in a well-worn navy suit. It was June, the train windows would be open and hot cinders from the locomotive tended to fly in and burn holes in one's clothing. She sent a lorry to the station with her trunk, but before catching the Philadelphia train she felt the need to stop at the Presbyterian Church of Falling Spring and ask for traveling mercies. She could walk to the station and she had plenty of time.

The church, a simple stone structure with two corner towers, a vaulted roof and stained glass windows, had served her family for generations. She shoved the heavy oak door open and stepped quietly into the silence. The walls were painted parchment white, the numbered family pews polished to a high shine and secured with white half-doors. Amanda walked down the side aisle to #72, the Kennedy pew, and sat down. The air was chilled with a slightly earthy, musty smell. She knelt and bowed her head.

At peace with herself and her decision Amanda resumed her walk to the station. The passenger platform was crowded with men sitting in rockers reading the morning papers. She opened her pocket watch and glanced at the time. She still had an hour before the train left. Directly across King Street from the station was a restaurant teeming with people, employees of the railroad and nearby Commonwealth Woolen Mill. Perfect. There was time for a quick breakfast.

After a hearty meal of sausage and eggs, she purchased her ticket, boarded the south bound train, and found an empty window seat. She eager for the journey ahead. George had said she was a stoic and spoke of the passive acceptance of fate, but she didn't really have a passive personality. She liked being in control of her life. She wanted to steer her own course. With her chin thrust forward she settled into her seat and pulled the latest issue of *Cosmopolitan* magazine from her reticule. It was a new woman's magazine featuring essays, articles and fiction. One article in particular interested her. It was entitled *The Emergence of Women in Society*. Amanda smiled. Apparently she was not alone in her quest for equality.

After many train changes Amanda reached Brunswick where she boarded a ferry to the island. The June sun had reached its zenith, the morning already scorching hot, as Amanda secured a lorry at the dock on St. Simons. She was proud of herself. The island was not an easy place to reach and she had maneuvered all of the transportation transfers without a hitch.

She could hardly wait to see the surprise on Michael's face when she appeared on his doorstep.

As the carriage rolled through the gates and up the wide entrance lane to McKenzie Resort she was amazed at the finished beauty of the grounds. Gone were all traces of hurricane damage. The white shell lane wound past numerous rose beds, then through a large rustic arbor covered with honeysuckle and ivy. A pomegranate hedge boarded a green lawn where a wide spreading chinaberry tree and a cluster of palm trees stood sentinel. Pink and white begonias spilled from flower boxes on the front veranda. The hotel looked like the old plantation home it had once been. Tables for outdoor dining were clustered next to a set of French doors that Amanda remembered opened into the formal dining room. At one of the tables Michael sat beside a beautiful young girl. Their heads were close together—very close together—and they were laughing at something.

At the sound of the horse and carriage Michael sprang to his feet and started across the veranda. Amanda was close enough to see the emotions sweep across his face as he recognized her. Shock, joy, confusion and, if she were not mistaken, a smidgeon of guilt. He turned his head to glance at the girl then back to her.

"Amanda!" he cried. He ran across the porch and down the steps.

As she alighted from the carriage he enfolded her in his arms. "I received no post that you were coming," he stammered.

"It was a hasty decision. I did not write. Oh, Michael, I'm glad to see you but . . ."

"But what?"

She glanced at the girl watching them intently. "I shouldn't have come upon you, unannounced."

Michael noticed Amanda's look and hurriedly said, "Come,

let me introduce you to Alica, the girl I hired to help with the reservations and act as hostess for the grand opening. Remember, I wrote you about her."

"I remember," Amanda said. What she didn't say was that bit of news had helped motivate her hasty trip.

After lifting her trunk from the carriage and dismissing the driver Michael tucked her hand into his and led her up the steps and over to the table where the girl waited.

"This is my fiancée, Amanda Kennedy. Amanda . . . Alica Bellefont," he said.

Amanda felt a wave of jealousy as they politely smiled at each other. The girl was everything she was not. Slim for one thing. And young, more than likely in her teens or early twenties. A cascade of black curls framed a heart shaped face with full pouting lips, an olive complexion and dark eyes hinting at a Creole heritage. After a few solicitous remarks about the weather and Amanda's trip she excused herself and headed indoors.

"Has she commenced work, already?" Amanda asked.

"Not really, but she has a room here."

"Oh."

"Room and board is part of her compensation."

"I see."

"I detect a hint of disapproval in your tone. Dang it, Amanda, it was you who changed our plans once again and necessitated my hiring her." His dark eyes flashed with annoyance. "And I still don't have a clue what your plans are. Now, let me find James and have him take your trunk up to one of the guest rooms. I'll tell Matilda to prepare an early lunch here on the veranda so we can sit and talk."

"I'd like to freshen up first."

"Of course." He grinned "Don't take too long though . . . I'm bursting with questions."

• • •

Within the hour Amanda had settled herself on the veranda in a
rocker next to his. A welcome sea-breeze ruffled his hair and a
blue-black crow swooped close to the table cawing loudly. They
began with small talk as Michael asked about Ford and Abby.
Amanda chattered at length about her trip to Johnstown and
Esther's miraculous rescue. The heat was stifling. They wiped
perspiration and swatted at sand fleas frequently as they talked.

"Reservations have been coming in at a rapid pace," Michael
said. "We are full for the opening and well into the winter season." He discussed the hotel for a few more minutes. Then there
was silence as each prepared for the more difficult discussion
ahead. Michael drummed his fingers on the table, a habit he had
when nervous. He directed his dark gaze to her face. "Enough
small talk. We have far more important things to talk about. "I
didn't see much luggage. Are you here to stay or is this just
another visit?"

Amanda didn't miss the sarcasm. *Oh dear. How was she to
answer that question?* Her fingers plucked at a pleat in her skirt.
Michael was a good person. The adversities he had overcome
had reinforced the show of strength in his face. Most women
would be drawn to him for his manliness, his gentleness, and the
sparkle in his black eyes. Why, then, was she hesitating?

There was silence, save for the cawing of the crows while she
tried to formulate an answer.

Michael reached over and clasped her hand. "Amanda, have
you changed your mind? Found someone you love better than
me? If so break it to me gently."

Changed her mind? She was not wavering for want of love.
She had loved Michael since childhood. Only her restlessness
had grown—her need to assert her individuality. She raised her
gaze from their clasped hands and looked intently into his eyes.

"When I saw you with Alica this morning I thought it was
you who had found someone else."

"Alica? She is only an employee . . . the designer I originally hired to help with the furnishings. Work you could have done had you been here. Look Amanda, it was you who created this situation when you placed your priorities elsewhere." He squeezed her hand so tightly her engagement ring cut deeply into her finger.

"I have never stopped loving you," she said. "It is only my needs that have changed."

"Needs? I don't understand. Tell me what I must do to make you marry me."

"Oh Michael . . . don't you see? It's just that women are beginning to fill a vital spot in society. They are fighting for equal rights, for the franchise to vote, to own property in their own name. For individuality. And I want to be a part of that movement. I want to be more than just an extension of my husband. Can I still do that and be your wife?"

Michael smiled softly. "Of course, you can, Sweetheart. I've also matured in my thinking. I recognize that you have different goals from the average woman and I've grown to respect your distinctness. Two years ago you asked me for more time and I gave it to you. I'll admit I didn't understand your needs then, but I think I do now. Or were you just playing with my affection?"

"No, of course not," she said haltingly. "I'll admit I have been floundering, Michael. One part of me wants to settle for a simple life of love and marriage, of raising a family and making a home for you. But that darn restless itch of mine craves a part in the growing emancipation of women."

"What then? I need an answer. I gather you have some unspoken conditions."

"I want to become a social worker."

Michael's face showed confusion and a flush of anger. "That's a new one. Before or after you marry me?"

"After." She took a deep breath. "I need at least a year of nurses training to fit me for social work as a visiting nurse. Since I already have a college degree Bellevue Hospital will accept me to a one-year program starting in September. Michael, I would have taken the training in the North while I was waiting for you to finish the hotel, but you know I didn't have the money. I have been working two jobs—the Children's Aid Society and tutoring a private student at the college to save enough to pay for the nursing program.

"Where is Bellevue?"

"New York."

"New York! New York City?"

"Yes . . . but, I can check into the possibility of finding a hospital in Jacksonville. That would be closer."

"You mean we would have to live apart?"

"Only during the training period. After I graduate I would plan to initiate a program here on the island for a social worker. Oh Michael, there is such a need. You've seen the poverty. Freed slaves have no education and live in hovels thrown up after the war."

"But, I want you to be with me."

"We can work something out. Winter should be a slow time here on St. Simons. Maybe Uncle Ford would come down and run the hotel for a few months and you could come north. He is pretty much retired now and, after all, this was once his home. Please understand how important this is to me."

"Understand? That's a pretty tall order." He swept the hair back from his forehead, his eyes dark and smoldering. He rose to his feet and walked over to the porch railing which he gripped with white knuckles. He stood for what seemed like an eternity then turned and came back. He knelt beside her. "You did say *after*, didn't you?" he asked, his voice husky. "If you love me then I guess that is all I need to understand. My darling, if you will be my wife you can do whatever makes you happy. I too had a dream and you have patiently waited for me. I can do no less for you."

His warm breath caressed her cheek, the love on his face

overpowering in its intensity. She believed Michael did understand her need to prove herself but he would grow to resent her
if she put off marriage once again. And what would she gain?
Independence? A career? She might never have another love as
honest and true as his. Could she risk losing that love?

No. The choice was clear.

•   •   •

Michael sat back on his haunches and watched the emotions
play out on Amanda's face. She laughed, the troubled look gone,
her eyes moist with joy. "I love you with all my heart and I do
want to marry you. Now."

It wasn't the way he wanted it, but it could work. It was hard
for him to accept but he realized now that Amanda would never
be truly happy in a marriage where she was simply an extension
of him. She needed to be her own person. Could he live with
that? He loved her enough to try.

"The hotel opens in two weeks," he said. I'm not sure I can
handle that and a wedding at the same time, but I don't want to
tempt fate by waiting another minute to make you mine."

Amanda rolled her blue eyes. "I agree. We've already weathered a hurricane and a flood. Life is fragile. Who knows what
might happen next? Why don't we just go to the courthouse in
Brunswick and have the clerk perform a simple ceremony. If we
want to have a formal wedding later after things have settled
down . . . when I am a nurse and you are a successful resort
operator . . . we can do it up proper then."

"You would be happy with that?"

"I would. Mother, of course, will be furious. She will suspect
all sorts of evil things which we must be careful not to let
happen. Eliza and Erin will be disappointed. I promised them
they could be flower girls. Aunt Abby will understand. She is as
non-traditional as I am."

"I don't think we have to go to Brunswick. There is a retired minister from the Brunswick Presbyterian Church here on the island. He has an office in his home on Frederica Road. It would be more personal than the courthouse . . . warmer and friendlier.

"I like that. Oh, let's do it Michael. When?"

His eyes were steady on hers. "Just as soon as I can make arrangements."

•   •   •

Two days later everything was in order, the wedding set for noon the next day. Amanda slept little that night. Getting married! She was getting married! What was she thinking? She had almost convinced herself she would never marry. She tossed and turned—considering her options. She had loved Michael all her life and she was keenly aware that it was now or never. He had agreed to let her enter the nurses training program. What more could she ask? She wondered if every girl was as full of conflicting emotions before her wedding.

The sun rose at last and she left her bed to sort through her wardrobe. She had not planned to get married, had brought no suitable frock. The mauve silk with mother-of-pearl buttons on a fitted bodice would have to do. It was a little out of date but it did have a small bustle in the back and a short train. She could only imagine her mother's horror if she learned that her daughter had not been dressed properly. Well, her mother was in for a lot of surprises.

Amanda spent an inordinate amount of time with her hair. The center part she had always worn disappeared and she swept the hair straight up from her face to the crown of her head in an elaborate pompadour, fully exposing her ears for the first time. Carefully she attached long, pendant earrings she had purchased in New York and never worn. A dab of pink salve gave subtle color to her lips. At last, satisfied with her appearance, she picked up her little purse and closed the door to her room. She had not thought to ask Michael what room they would be sharing as husband and wife. She must tell him to instruct Matilda where to move her belongings for tonight.

He was waiting for her in the entrance hall and she gave a little gasp of pleasure when she saw him. He wore what looked like a new black suit and a white shirt with boned collar that reached to just under his chin. How dashing he was. His skin was a golden bronze, his black hair and eyes gleamed, he stood tall, proud and straight as a warrior.

"I bought the suit for the opening," he said, self-consciously tugging at his jacket and adjusting the knees of his trousers. "They have a new store in Brunswick that sells ready-made clothing."

"You look grand."

"And so do you. I've never seen you with your hair that way." He winked at her. "I've never seen your ears."

"Thank you. I don't usually do it so fancy" She grinned. "But this is a special day."

Michael took her arm and led her into the dining room. He pulled a chair from the table with a flourish. "We have time for a quick breakfast," he said as Matilda moved to her side.

"Just a cup of tea and a biscuit, please. I'm too nervous to eat."

"Well, I'm hungry. I'll have a bowl of grits and some bacon, Matilda. And coffee. Oh, and we won't be home tonight. I've asked James to prepare the new phaeton. I thought Amanda and I would drive to Savannah for a nice dinner at a hotel. We will spend the night and return tomorrow." He smiled at Amanda. "I realize it is a short honeymoon but with the opening so close I have a dozen last minute details to take care of. I promise I'll make it up to you later."

"Savannah sounds lovely," Amanda said. "I understand." What she didn't quite understand is why he hadn't discussed his plans with her.

• • •

Michael turned the carriage off Frederica Road and followed a sandy lane leading to Reverend Quiner's home. It sat along winding Vassar Creek, bordering a wide expanse of marsh. The grounds were unbelievably beautiful. Huge, hundred-year-old oak trees swept their branches across a manicured lawn. Amanda knew immediately that she wanted to be married under one of those fantastic trees.

Reverend Quiner met them at the door and showed them into his study to the right of the entrance hall. He was a portly gentleman with dark hair shot with gray and a ruddy complexion. As they entered the room a gray-haired lady rose to greet them. She was a tall woman with a rather horsey face, and stood a good inch higher than the rest of them.

"My wife, Mrs. Quiner," the pastor said by way of introduction. "She will be our witness. Now, if you will move over here in front of the fireplace I'll get my robe and bible and we can begin."

Amanda smiled. "Reverend, it is such a lovely day and your grounds are so beautiful . . . do you think we could say our vows outside?"

The pastor nodded his head. "Of course, my dear, if that is what you want. Mother, take them out back while I gather my things. I'll join you there."

They exited from a door at the rear of the study and stepped into bright sunlight. It only took minutes for Amanda to spot the place she wanted the ceremony to take place.

Two towering live oaks stood framed against the creek where an egret stepped regally in search of food. Behind it gold-tipped marsh grass swayed in a slight breeze against a blue sky. Several massive branches of the live oak swooped to the ground, almost touching the earth before sweeping upward. It had rained yesterday and curly green resurrection fern, signifying new life, covered the tree's bark. Amanda strode purposely across the lawn to stand before one of the branches, facing the marsh and sea beyond. "This is it," she said taking Michael's hand.

The pastor and Mrs. Quiner joined them with a smile of approval. As Reverend Quiner opened his Bible Michael spoke up, his face flushed. "Sir, I have no ring. There isn't a jeweler on the island and I didn't have a chance to go to the mainland to purchase one. Can we skip that part of the ceremony?"

The pastor hesitated, his heavy eyebrows drawn together. "Rings are largely ceremonial, but important." He glanced at his wife. A smile softened her stern features as she twisted her wedding ring from her finger and handed it to her husband. Amanda wondered how many times this kind woman had done the same thing for nervous young couples.

Reverend Quiner nodded in satisfaction as he handed the ring to Michael. "You can return it after the service," he said. "Let us begin."

Solemnly they repeated the marriage vows but when they came to the words "trust and obey," Amanda hesitated briefly. Dared she insert her own words? Michael looked at her in alarm.

She could not be a rebel. Not today. She cleared her throat and repeated the words softly with only a slight hitch in her voice.

•   •   •

The sun was setting in the west when Michael pulled the coach to a stop before the Pirate's Cove Hotel on Savannah's river-front.

"Will this do, honey?" he asked.

"It's perfect. See if they have a room available with a view of the harbor."

Michael hid a smile. He didn't plan on spending much time looking out a window.

•   •   •

After settling into the Honeymoon Suite they went down to the elegant dining room for dinner. Michael ordered a bottle of champagne and after offering a toast to his new bride they drank leisurely, enjoying the ambience of the elegant old hotel. He couldn't keep his eyes off the profile of his new wife, her strong chin, her straight nose, her delicate ears. She was gracious, poised, self-assured. And every bit a woman. The wine gave him a slight buzz and as they lingered over their drinks he spent most of his time watching the rise and fall of her breasts against the creamy silk of her bodice. *I must go slow*, he kept reminding himself. *I want to relish every minute of this night.*

After a delicious dinner of smoked salmon they ordered dessert. And coffee. That was encouraging. Amanda wasn't worried about being kept awake.

The waiter came by and presented the check. Michael examined it with a gulp, then dropped some bills on the table and glanced at Amanda.

"Shall we retire to our room, Mrs. McKenzie?"

She looked at him coyly, the wine flushing her face. "I thought you would never get around to asking, Mr. McKenzie."

He took her in his arms and kissed her as soon as the door was closed. It was a long kiss. They were both adults now. All grown up. This time there would be no immature fumbling on a dark beach. His conscience demanded he take his time. He slid one hand into her hair, pulling it loose from its pins, while his other hand pressed into the small of her back pulling her tight against him. Her eyes were closed and she began to sway against him. The kiss went on and on—slow and deep and very satisfying.

Perhaps they both realized that a wedding night only happens once. That it should create a memory they could savor forever.

When the kiss ended they were still just beyond the door. Amanda ran her tongue over swollen lips and he could feel her heart pounding against his chest. She moved her hand to the buttons on his shirt.

"No, I want to undress you, first," he said.

Her mouth quirked in a smile and she said, "Be careful. This is the only good dress I have with me."

"Where do I start?"

"In the back. With that row of buttons."

They joined together in another kiss as his fingers sought to undo the mother-of-pearl buttons marching up her back. They were tiny—and slippery—and his fingers were large and clumsy. When he made it to the top she held out her arms and he undid the buttons on the leg-of-mutton sleeves. The silk fell back from her wrists and he pulled the dress forward letting it fall to the floor.

The kiss ended and they pulled apart. "Now I know why women have maids," he mumbled. "It must take hours to get you into and out of your clothing."

She laughed. "Just wait. The rest is even more complicated."

More buttons, more kisses, then Amanda stepped out of a puddle of silk and taffeta. "My turn," she said as she began to unbutton his shirt, starting at the top and working her way sensuously down his chest. They kissed again, still slow, the anticipation building. Michael's hand dropped to his side and he unbuttoned his pants. He eased his shirt out of the waistband. Amanda tilted her head back and looked deep into his eyes. He reached down and with a slight tug his pants slid over his hips. She looked down. Her eyes widened. Then she smiled.

They were both in their undergarments, still in the hall. Amanda's breasts swelled above the cups of her camisole, her skin the color of ripe peaches. Michael's need became more urgent and he took her hand, stepped over their clothing, and led her towards the bed.

"Wait, Michael," she whispered. "Let me finish undressing in private and get into a gown."

"Then, hurry. I've been waiting for this moment far too long."

He lit several candles in the room, then sat down on the edge of the bed, removed his shoes, socks, and underdrawers, and waited.

Amanda stepped from behind the screen. She had not donned a gown and the candlelight washed her skin with gold. She tossed her head, her rich auburn hair cascading over her shoulders. Her breasts were magnificent.

Michael felt like throwing her to the floor and taking her right there. But he reminded himself of his resolve to go slowly. He rose and stood silently, his arms stretched out to receive her as she walked toward him.

They kissed once more, their lips clinging together as he eased her onto the bed. Michael lay facing her, looking deep into her blue eyes. He pushed the hair away from her ear and kissed it. Then she kissed his, teasing her tongue in his eardrum. The sensation almost made him lose control. She toyed with the hair on his chest and his hand massaged her nipples. They were sensitive and he felt her shudder. They spent five delicious moments getting to know each others bodies. Then he could wait no longer. He started tenderly, he did not want to hurt her. He heard her gasp and stiffen and then she began to relax and move with him.

This time it was as it should be. Not just sex but an act of love between a man and his wife.

Afterward, Amanda slipped out of the tumbled feather bed and donned the gown she had let lie behind the privacy screen in an impulsive defiance of convention. She climbed back in bed beside her husband and they lay quietly, snuggled together, holding hands. Amanda shifted her position and Michael's arm went around her. She rested her head on his chest and laughed when the hair tickled her nose.

"I see you put on a gown," he commented.

"I felt funny naked."

"I liked it."

They fell quiet again, content in their closeness. Amanda was almost asleep when Michael said, "we should stop to see my grandmother tomorrow. She will be delighted to hear of our marriage. She still has not sold her home. The economy has been bad and she is beginning to be afraid she will die before realizing her dream of returning to St. Simons. She wants to build a cottage on the north end of the plantation, but I want to urge her to move into one of the rooms in the hotel on a permanent basis."

"How old is she now?"

"Seventy-four." He hesitated. "You know she borrowed money on the equity of her home here in Savannah to help me finish my education and rebuild. I couldn't have done it without her. Free room and board is one way I could start to repay her."

"Then by all means, let's stop. I can add reinforcements to your argument." Amanda chuckled. "I will tell her I need someone to keep an eye on you while I'm gone."

Michael pulled her tighter, almost smothering her. "Don't talk about leaving me," he grumbled. "After tonight, I'll never let you go."

She thought about that for a minute. Then she decided not to comment. They said nothing more about nightgowns, or rooms for a grandmother, or schools, or professions. And then they fell asleep in each others arms, in the still quiet peace of a Georgia night.

Chapter Eleven

The scent of salt water wafted into her room as Amanda dressed for the grand opening. Reluctantly she had asked a busy Matilda to come up from the kitchen to help her with her corset. First she donned a silk chemise, two petticoats, and knee-length stockings, then Matilda helped to place and pull the corset tight. Amanda had definitely put on more weight and vowed to watch her diet. Together they lowered a cream silk gown over her head and Matilda secured the long row of buttons. With that done she released Matilda who needed to get back to her duties in the kitchen. Amanda thought, *I'll either have to wear clothing I can dress in myself or hire a maid. The poor woman can't be both cook and wait on me.* She worked on her hair herself, pulling it back from her forehead and piling it on top in a psyche knot. Dabbing scent on her wrists and smiling jauntily, she opened the door and started down the stairs to greet the first guests.

Michael, clean-shaven, his freshly-cut black hair parted in the middle, was already at the front desk conversing with a young couple with two small children. He handed them their key, motioned to James to carry their luggage to their room and introduced his wife as the hotel hostess. Her face radiant with good cheer, Amanda showed them the dining room and explained the dinner hours.

Within hours the lobby was swarming with guests and chaos. Children ran back and forth to the beach tracking sand onto the gleaming floors. Several little boys had delighted in bursting all of the balloons festooning the veranda and an irate peacock had pecked the hand of a young girl when she tried to pet it. Amanda was beginning to wonder if it would always be like this. By the end of the day both she and Michael were exhausted. Finally Michael was able to lock the front door and they retreated to the kitchen for a hasty supper. A weary Matilda was still cleaning up the dishes and James was helping her.

"Well, now we know what running a resort hotel is like," Michael said.

Amanda sighed. "Surely, it won't always be this hectic."

"No, some days it likely be worse," James grumbled.

Amanda reached down to loosen her front-laced shoes from swollen ankles. "Thank heavens you retained Alica to take care of the bookkeeping and money. I don't think I could even write my name tonight."

Wearily they climbed the stairs to their own room and within minutes they were in bed. Amanda lay next to him and turned her back. Michael blew out the lamp and put his hand on her hip. For the first time since their wedding night she didn't respond.

•   •   •

First light had just broken across the cloud-scudded sky above McKenzie Resort when Michael rolled out of bed. He reminded himself that he had to be fully dressed in a business suit, not a bathrobe, when he appeared downstairs. Quietly he shaved and dressed, careful not to wake Amanda who was sleeping soundly.

Matilda was already in the kitchen preparing for the expected breakfast crowd. "The tables be all set up, ober in the dinin' room," she said, handing him a mug of steaming coffee. "Don' you be messin' 'em up."

Michael grinned. "I guess that means I'm relegated to the kitchen for my breakfast from now on."

Matilda simply rolled her big black eyes and continued to cut a huge slab of bacon into thick strips for frying.

Michael carried his coffee out to the veranda where James

was busy wiping dew from the rockers. Most of the guests had arrived the day before but two couples were expected today. A bright sun was already burning off the early morning fog. Thank heavens it wasn't raining. He reminded himself that one of the advantages of a seaside resort was that he was not required to provide man-made entertainment. The beach and ocean were already there.

•   •   •

By the time Amanda awoke the sun was streaming through windows open to the sound of lapping surf and rustling wind. It had to be very late, she thought, feeling for Michael beside her. He wasn't there! She reached out to her nightstand, lifted the lid on her pocket watch and looked at the time. A quarter past seven. Breakfast was at eight and her presence at the dining room table was expected. She sighed. She was not a gregarious person by nature and already she was feeling the pressure of being a smiling hostess.

She dressed hurriedly in a simple shirtwaist but before starting down to the dining room she walked over to a white wicker writing desk and picked up the letter she intended to post today requesting information about a nurses' training school in Philadelphia. It was a possibility if nothing materialized in the South. Just handling the letter made her feel better about the day ahead. Another letter, this one addressed to her mother, also lay on the table waiting to be posted. In it she explained her sudden marriage to Michael and asked Sarah to clean out her room and ship her clothes and personal belongings to St. Simons.

Several more letters had to be written—one to Mr. Orr at the Children's Aid Society telling him to submit her resignation to the Board. She was married and would definitely not be coming bacck. Harder yet, one to the matron asking her to explain to Bobby that Amanda would be staying in Georgia. She hoped it would be done compassionately. Then she must write to George telling him of her marriage. Amanda chewed her lip. It would be a difficult letter to write. She knew he would be hurt and disappointed.

•   •   •

Meanwhile, back in Chambersburg, Amanda's Aunt Abby climbed the set of stone steps cut into a bank leading from the spring house to a broad stretch of lawn at her home on Falling Spring Road. She stepped carefully, aware of the damp moss that always clung to the stone and had caused her to fall several times. Once across the slope of lawn, she made for a doorway tucked into the side wall and let herself into the kitchen.

The grandfather clock in the parlor was chiming the hour and she headed straight for the stairwell to climb to her bedroom and begin dressing for dinner. She had just come from the hatchery to remind Ford that they had a six o'clock reservation at the Graeffenburg Inn. Today was their twenty-fourth wedding anniversary.

She had finished bathing when she heard her husband approach, his footsteps resolute on the pine floorboards.

Ford paused in the doorway his gaze traveling slowly over her half-dressed body then he crossed the room to take her in his arms. "You are as beautiful today as you were the first time I saw you," he said. His hands slid down her back and he pulled her close against him. He kissed her, deeply and fully, then gave her a wicked wink and whispered, "Have we time, do you think?"

Abby pulled away with an engaging laugh. "Hardly. I believe you better save it for dessert."

"I'll scarcely taste my dinner in anticipation."

Dinner that night was at the Graeffenburg Inn, seven miles east of Chambersburg in the beautiful pine woodland called Caledonia. The original Log Cabin Tavern had been built in the early 1800s by Alexander Caldwell to serve the Conestoga wagons traveling the Pittsburgh Turnpike. Three days before the Battle of Gettysburg, General Jubal Early burned the Tavern. It was later rebuilt and named Graeffenburg after an old spa in Austria. Now, it was a well known resort with mineral springs said to cure various ailments. It had two bath houses with apartments on the second floor and mineral pools beneath. The socially prominent from New York, Philadelphia and Baltimore made annual visits to the spa in early spring and fall. Its restaurant was small but said to be the best in Franklin County.

"I believe a drink is in order," Ford said as he accepted a menu from the waiter. "Rum and tonic, on ice with a lemon twist." He glanced at Abby.

"I'll have Madeira, please," she said studiously studying the menu.

She settled on the Baked Stuffed Brook Trout with a filling of rice, bread crumbs, herbs, cream and white wine. Ford chose Braised Round of Beef with brandied mushroom gravy.

"What do you think of Michael and Amanda's marriage?" Abby asked as they sipped their drinks.

"I hope they didn't do something that made them feel they had to get married."

"Oh, Ford, I hardly think that is the answer."

"He's a man, isn't he, and he has been waiting for a long time. Pressures build up." He winked. "As well we both know."

"Well, I think Amanda finally gave up the idea of a career and settled for marriage and a family. If the family is already started, I'll not fault her."

Ford finished his drink and ordered another. Abby gave him a worried look. "The horse knows the way home," he said with a grin. A candle on the table cast golden light on his graying copper hair brushed back from a face remarkably free of wrinkles. "Don't worry about Michael and Amanda, Honey. They have both traveled a hard road and I'm sure it has made them stronger for it. They will be all right."

The waiter arrived with their dinner and for the next few minutes they were busy with napkins and silverware.

"Um, delicious," Abby said as she delved into her fish. "I wonder if this trout came from our hatchery."

"Could be."

They ate slowly, making small talk about the recent drought, labor's fight for an eight-hour day, the aftermath of the Haymarket bombing, and the country's slow economic recovery from the Panic of '73.

"I spoke with Esau this morning," Ford said, "and I told him we would like to go to St. Simons for several weeks this winter. He agreed to care for the farm and hatchery while we are gone but I sensed some reluctance on his part."

"What do you mean?"

"More and more Esau seems to be physically hampered by rheumatism. He mentioned just last week that he might have to stop working at the hatchery because of the water and dampness." Ford ran his fingers through his thinning hair. "I guess we are both getting old."

Abby laughed. "Not you. You are as handsome and viral as ever."

"Remember that viral part."

"I always do."

"But, Abby, I would be lost without him. We have been together since childhood—always more than master and slave—our roles circumscribed by our culture. My father gave him to me as a manservant when I reached puberty and he became my right hand, an extension of me in everything I did. As you know he followed me into the great war and when I offered him his freedom he declined saying his place was by my side. It was only after the war that he accepted his freedom."

Abby pursed her lips. "I'll admit I have never understood your acceptance of slavery. It was abhorrent to me when I first met you. Totally unlike the kind, caring nature of the man I grew to love."

"But a way of life I was raised to believe was necessary in the South. Not all slaves were treated like those in *Uncle Tom's Cabin*. My father never sold off family members. Esau's father was our coachman until he died, his mother our cook. My mother taught Esau to read."

"Still, they were slaves."

"I know that and I realize it wasn't right." Ford's face grew pensive. "I have been thinking about giving up the hatchery. It isn't that profitable anymore, and you and I are deserving of a slower pace in this last chapter of our lives."

"Give up the hatchery!"

Ford nodded. "And some of the farm work. I could lease some acreage to our neighbor, Mr. Lehman. He told me some time ago that he might be interested. It would give us more freedom. I would like to be free to travel to St. Simons more often, especially to help my mother move to the island after she sells her house in Savannah. And I could relieve Esau of his feeling of obligation to continue to work here. Maybe give him a small stipend just to look after things while we are gone."

Abby crossed her arms and sighed. "I guess you are right but I don't . . ." her voice trailed off.

"Don't what?"

"Don't like the phrase 'last chapter of our lives.' Or 'old.'" She laughed. "I don't feel old."

Ford reached across the table and took her hand. "You aren't and I shouldn't have put it that way. But Sweetheart we need to slow down, to enjoy the fruits of our years of hard work and sacrifice. To still dream."

A slow smile spread across Abby's face. "Then sell the hatchery, Ford."

"I will talk to Esau again. I think he will be relieved. Now enough talk. Let's concentrate on this excellent dinner."

The sun was beginning to set in the west when the waiter arrived to take their plates. "Are we having dessert tonight," he asked.

Ford winked at Abby and she smiled. "No thank you. I believe we are having dessert at home tonight."

Ford had just turned the carriage off the Pike onto Falling Spring Road when they heard the loud clanging of a fire truck. Within minutes the horse-drawn apparatus of the Friendship Engine and Hose Company charged past them.

"I smell smoke," Abby said.

"So do I . . . look you can see a glow in the sky ahead. Dang, that must be close to our place." He snapped the reins to speed up their carriage. Another clanging fire truck was coming up behind them and the smell of smoke grew stronger. As they pulled even with Cider Press Road they saw flames illuminating the night sky. High atop a hill they saw the fire. It was their barn.

They got as close as they could. Apparatus from both the Goodwill Hose Company and the Cumberland Valley Hose Company was choking the driveway. Ford vaulted from the carriage. "Stay here and control the horse," he yelled as he ran toward the burning barn.

His legs flew across the lawn which sloped uphill from the creek and spring house, his heart pounding against his ribs. The air echoed with shouting men and clanging fire engines still arriving on the scene. Black clouds of smoke billowed from the burning barn and bright points of flame danced in the darkness. The barn was completely engulfed as was the field behind it. Hoses pumping water direct from the creek snaked uphill, water hissed loudly raising clouds of steam. Ford paused, gulping thick air. His legs trembled, his nose burned and his throat was raw. He prayed that all of the cattle housed in the stanchions had escaped. He could hear a bawling cow from within and started to run toward the burning barn when a hand grabbed him and pulled him back.

"No use, Mr McKenzie," the fireman shouted. "We got most of 'em out." He waved to the north field where Ford could make out shapes moving about in the dark.

"Thank God," Ford groaned.

"Here comes the Friendship's new LaFrance steamer," a man yelled as another fire truck charged into view pulled by a lathered horse.

The fireman let go of Ford's sleeve and wiped his grimy, soot-covered face. "Started as a brush fire in that field runs along the railroad tracks," he said. "It's tinder dry from the recent drought and the train running to Greencastle had just passed through. I suppose sparks from the locomotive set it afire."

"Damn railroad," Ford spat. "Everyone knows how I fought to keep it off my farm. Now look what has happened." He brushed sweat-soaked hair from his forehead with a trembling hand as he turned and strode back to the carriage to consol Abby. Tears ran down her face as she held tight rein on their agitated horse.

"The cows?"

"I was told most of them are safe." He put his arms around her and held her tight. "It started as a brush fire, probably from a passing train. The barn is gone and they are directing water on the house. I don't think it is in danger."

"Then we have much to be thankful for," she said. The fire could have traveled to the house while we were asleep. The livestock are safe and we are safe. The barn can be rebuilt."

Ford stepped back and stared at her in wonder. What an unsinkable spirit this remarkable woman had. Here he was raging at fate while she was only thankful. How had he ever been lucky enough to marry a woman like her?

• • •

Michael was sorting the mail—reservations, requests for information, bills in one pile—personal letters in another. He hesitated and turned one envelope over to look at it a second time.

"It's for you Amanda. The return address is Dr. George Cochran. Isn't that Esther's brother?"

Amanda felt an unexpected tremble in her fingers as she took the letter. "Yes, it is. I hope it isn't bad news about her. She's been doing so well." She took the envelope and tucked it into her pocket.

Michael's brow puckered. "Aren't you going to read it?"

"It's hot in here. I'll take it out to the veranda where there is a breeze and I can be more comfortable. Is there anything else for me?"

"No." He picked up several envelopes. "Will you stay here at the desk for a few minutes while I take these in to Alica?"

"I can take them to her on my way out."

He had a queer look on his face as he handed her the mail. "Fine. Ask her to join us for lunch. I have a few things I need to discuss."

As she walked away with the mail in her hand she wondered if both of them were trying to hide something.

Amanda settled herself in a comfortable rocker and began to read George's letter:

Yesterday I received your message telling me of your marriage. I must say it left me with a heavy heart. It should come as no surprise that I was hoping for a different outcome, but I hope we can remain friends.

*I have thought several times about the young boy—
Bobby, I believe his name was—with the harelip. I would
like to take on the surgical challenge to fix it. I'll admit to
a feeling of a moral responsibility to perhaps change the
direction of his life. In fact the humane effect of reconstructive surgery is why I am making it my speciality. It
should be very rewarding. Will you please tell me to whom
I should write at the Children's Aid Society? My services
in this instance would be free.*

*Esther has resumed a normal life and little Ruth is
grow-ing fat and sassy.*

I wish you much happiness, Amanda.
Your friend,
George.

With a deep sigh she returned the letter to its envelope and
put it back in her pocket.

Amanda was disappointed to find that there were no hospitals in
the South that offered the training she sought. The newest and
most promising were all in large Northern cities—Bellevue in
New York, Massachusetts General in Boston, Johns Hopkins in
Baltimore and Pennsylvania Hospital in Philadelphia. Michael
was more than disappointed. He was devastated.

"You can't leave me and go away for two years," he
grumbled as they lay side by side in bed. "That's asking too
much."

"Bellevue has written that they have an accelerated program
for college graduates, allowing students a one year program."

"That is still a year of separation. We just got married."

"Be reasonable, Michael. Think of all the times men go off to
war and leave their wives and children. They can be gone for

years at a time."

"It's that important to you?"

"It is. You know it is. We can work something out. Write Uncle Ford and ask him if he and Aunt Abby could come down for a month or two to take care of the resort. Maybe in January and February. That way I will be well started at school and we can get a room together." Amanda's face brightened. "Maybe we could stay with Esther's grandmother, she has extra bedrooms and George is no longer staying with her."

"Have you had any replies from other schools?"

"Three replied and offered me admittance but they are two-year programs. All are new to the idea of training nurses and anxious to build their student body. I especially like Bellevue because Lavinia Dock is working there and I've told you how much I admire her."

"When would you start?"

"September."

Michael sighed and drew Amanda to him. "Enough talk. I want you tonight, sweetheart."

Without hesitation her arms went around his neck. She seemed as eager as he. In the golden glow of the lamp, he leaned over her and removed her gown. He murmured endearments in her tiny ear and they found a rhythm that carried them both to fulfillment.

The next morning Amanda woke to find Michael on his elbow staring at her intently.

"Did you know you snore?" he said.

"I do not."

"You do." He tweaked her nose. "But I love it. It's a cute snore."

She slapped him playfully. He snuggled up against her and they lay in each others arms, content just to be close.

"Michael," Amanda whispered, breaking the silence, "Can I ask you something?"

"What, dear?"

"Were you ever intimate with Alica?"

A red flush crept up his face. He did not answer.

"Michael . . . ?"

"I'll not lie to you. When you chose to go to Johnstown I was angry and hurt. I thought you no longer loved me, that you wanted to break our engagement."

"I came as soon as I could," she said, her voice cold as death." Her stomach was churning, her face hot and pinched with resentment. "How could you?"

"It only happened once."

"But you have kept her on. How can I believe you when she still works and lives at the lodge?"

"I'll let her go. Honestly, Amanda, it was before you came back and we were married. I would never be unfaithful to you now. Men are human and the sexual urge is strong. We all make mistakes."

Ah, that is the problem, Amanda thought contritely. *How close had she come to making a mistake with George?* Tears filled her eyes. She felt betrayed, sullied, her ego bruised. Yet, she had read enough to know that men looked at sex differently than women. Could she really have believed that he would remain chaste and wait for her all of the years she chose to stay away.

"I'm sorry, dear," he said, his voice soft and urgent. "I never meant you to know. I never meant to hurt you."

Amanda sat up and moved to the side of the bed. "Give me time, Michael. Time to sort out my feelings. I think I understand and I'll try to find forgiveness. Just give me time."

Amanda's stomach had been tied in knots since Michael's morning confession. She wished she had not asked him about Alica, but she had. Now she had to live with his answer. Her relief when she had a problem had always been to take a walk alone, to ponder her feelings in the silence of solitude and allow her mind to dwell on the issue at hand. Accordingly, after breakfast she set off down the beach toward the village.

A heavy fog bank hung close to the ground, only the lap of the surf revealing the nearby sea. She sought out a flight of weathered stairs leading from a cottage to the beach and settled herself on a wooden step still wet from the receding tide. Her inward ear listened to a distant echo of two young people sitting on similar steps eager for the fire of love and life. Much had happened since then to mold them into mature adults.

She could forgive Michael his infidelity during their engagement. He had been confused by her continued absence while she vacillated between marriage and career. She understood that. She, herself, had felt the demon of temptation. She sat quietly in the stillness of early morning, her gaze moving over miles of sand and the endless ocean washed with shafts of sunlight. She was still troubled by the restlessness that was her nature, but she had never believed that one should be satisfied with tranquility. Human beings needed spirit in their lives or they became without purpose.

A gull's guttural cry jolted Amanda. It was perched on a piling, wings spread wide to dry, instinctively knowing what must be done before resuming its relentless search for sustenance. She jumped to her feet. What was done, was done. She had a busy day ahead of her including a trip to the mainland. Tonight she would let Michael know that he was forgiven.

But she would also let him know that there was to be no more nonsense about Alica. She had to go.

Chapter Twelve

 $\mathcal{F}$ rom the beginning of her quest for a training school Amanda knew that New York's Bellvue was uppermost in her heart. And in the end it was the one that prevailed.

The Bellevue Hospital Medical College was a daring experiment in the education of women. It was the first training school in the United States to operate under the Florence Nightingale principals established at St. Thomas's hospital in London. Opened in 1873, the Bellevue school was growing in reputation as one of the greats in the world. It offered women a new profession—previously reviled, ill paid, and without honor.

The sprawling buildings sat on the curving shoreline of Manhattan Island where Twenty-Sixth Street meets up with the East River. Their program allowed students to leave before the required two years were up if they could pay for their training and board and be subject to the hospital's rules and discipline. On these terms, they were free to leave the school at any time. This fit Amanda's agenda just fine.

For one year's training the charge was set at one hundred dollars for instruction and two hundred dollars for board. Amanda had some savings and when she wrote to tell her mother of her plans her step-father offered to fund the rest. Michael reluctantly agreed to her choice of New York. So on a morning early in September Amanda walked through the imposing brick gatehouse that led to Bellevue Hospital and its relatively new medical college for nurses.

She spent a busy first week getting settled at the Nurses

Home on East Twenty-Sixth Street, then purchasing her text book and paying a quick visit to O'ma at the Dakota. Now dressed in her blue-and-white-striped uniform and stiff freshman cap she entered the auditorium for her first lecture. She took her seat among dozens of chattering probies, aware that she might be the oldest student nurse there. Nervously, she adjusted her hair, smoothed her apron, and opened her new notebook. All fell quiet as the professor, Dr. Frank Walker, Professor of Surgery of Bones and Accidents, took his place at the lectern. His tall, straight figure with luxuriant side whiskers and beard above a very high white collar and black frockcoat was immediately reassuring.

The lecture lasted forty-five minutes, with fifteen minutes at the end given to questions. After the lecture Amanda found herself relaxed, eager to learn more, transported back in time to her college years at Wilson.

That evening she settled herself in a comfortable chair in the study parlor of the Nurses Home and opened her textbook, *The Manual of Nursing*. Eleven girls were seated either at the round mahogany table in the center of the room or in small clusters where animated conversation ebbed and flowed as they discussed their experiences that day. It was a cozy room with flocked wallpaper and numerous tall windows with white tie-back curtains opening onto the busy New York street. Gas lights cast a warm glow on the eager young faces of her classmates and Amanda closed her eyes in a silent prayer of thanksgiving that she had been given this opportunity to grow as a woman. She remembered reading somewhere that "to those of whom much had been given, God, the Giver, would expect much."

Her first month was spent attending classes and working in the wards. There were twelve wards under the care of the nursing school, each with a head nurse, all under the supervision of the

superintendent, Miss Agnes Brennan. Then, because of a
shortage of trained nurses and because of her age and education,
Amanda was told to take charge of night duty. Fortunately she
learned quickly, but she felt woefully ill-prepared to take charge
of anything and almost quit before she got started. She was
expected to become familiar with one hundred patients, to remember the names of each of the doctors and their specialities,
and to know where the supplies in each ward were kept.

Her stomach was tied in knots when she reported at seven-
thirty for her first tour of night duty, an eighteen-hour shift with
only one relief. Orders were oral, not written, and she reported
to the day nurse in charge of each ward, received her orders and
passed them on to the night nurses. When the day shift departed
the gas lights were turned so low she could barely see the faces
of the patients huddled in their gray blankets. Most of the
patients were from the Lower East Side, the slums of New York.
At first Amanda had to admit she was fearful and repulsed by
this class of people, ones she had never been among. Most of
them were filthy, profane or under the influence of stimulants.
But gradually her initial repulsion grew to profound pity for
their wretched poverty. She soon found among them an occasional pearl who made her know she had chosen the right
profession.

After working all night she was expected to attend classes and
lectures during the day. Fortunately, or unfortunately, she was
too tired most of the time to miss Michael. Then in November a
new policy was instituted that only trained, graduate nurses
would be in charge of the wards. Lectures with Bellevue's leading physicians were scheduled on a regular basis and classroom
work became more clinical in nature. This relieved Amanda of
night duty and returned her to student status.

Early in December O'ma invited Amanda to take tea with Mrs.

Schuylar, an original member of the group of women who were responsible for the actual formation of the Nursing School.

They were on their second cup of tea when Mrs. Schuylar turned to Amanda with a smile and said: "My dear you can't imagine the conditions that prevailed a scant fifteen years ago. When I walked through the wards of Bellevue Hospital with members of our Visiting Committee I saw at once that no permanent improvement could be made until the nursing service was radically changed and that this could only be accomplished through the establishment of a training school.

"I had never been in a hospital before and the sight of the patients and the loathsome smells sickened me so that I nearly fainted. The condition of the patients and the beds was unspeakable. The one nurse on duty slept in the bathroom and the tub was filled with filthy rubbish. It was on a Friday. The dinner of salt fish was brought to the ward in a burlap bag and spilled onto the table. The patients helped themselves and carried meals on tin plates to those who couldn't leave their beds. After seeing the kitchen our committee was taken into a large building which proved to be the laundry. Nauseous steam was rising from great cauldrons filled with filthy clothing, which one old pauper was stirring with a stick. He had no soap." Mrs. Schuylar grimaced. "I won't recount the conditions we found in the wards. You wouldn't be able to take pleasure in this delightful tea."

"It's hard to believe," Amanda said. "Everything seems so clean and well organized now."

"That is due to strict adherence to the Florence Nightingale principals and the excellent steerage of Sister Helen, the first superintendent of the school. You must remember that at that time Bellevue was New York's largest pauper hospital and before the training school was instituted it had no trained nurses. Do you plan to continue nursing here?"

"No. I am married and live in the South. I would really like to establish a Children's Aid Society on our island and do social work among the poor."

"Very commendable. My own idea of service to the suffering extends far beyond the public hospitals of New York. I envision an organization that will someday promote not only the care of the sick but the aged, the tubercular, the feeble-minded, and the insane."

O'ma passed the tray of tea sandwiches to Miss Schuylar. "I recently attended a fund-raiser where an appeal was made by a Miss Lillian Wald for funds to establish a settlement house on the Lower East Side," she said. "I am very interested in supporting the project and made a sizable donation."

"I met her at Johnstown," Amanda volunteered. "She's a Bellevue graduate."

Miss Schuylar nodded. "I understand she has secured a house and plans to open soon. It will be called the Henry Street Settlement and offer visiting nurses for the poor, as well as numerous social services. My, these sandwiches are delicious. May I have another?"

"Please do. I'll ring for more tea," O'ma said.

The afternoon passed all too quickly and Amanda basked in a feeling of wellbeing as the conversation turned to the suffrage movement, social reform, and the latest medical advances. She felt set on an honorable course and was proud of herself.

Michael wrote that the hotel was full for the holidays and he could not possibly leave to celebrate Christmas with her. Alica's employment had been terminated several months before and he was coping with all of work himself. Amanda was terribly disappointed, lonely and a little guilty. And just a bit worried about how he might choose to celebrate. Angrily she chastised herself. Full of contrition she volunteered to work Christmas Eve so her roommate could spend it with her parents.

In January she received a note from O'ma. George was going

to be in New York later in the month for a medical conference. He had something of importance he wished to discuss with Amanda and asked if she could come for dinner on the nineteenth. Thinking the matter probably involved Esther, she arranged to have that evening free and join them for a late supper. She arrived at the Dakota eager to see George and get a report on her friend. After taking her wraps the maid showed her into the sitting room. O'ma was sitting before a cheerful fire and jumped to her feet to enfold her in a warm hug. George placed a chaste kiss on her cheek.

"Sit down and join us in a glass of Madeira before we eat," O'ma said leading her to the couch.

"Thank you. I can use something to warm me up. It's bitter cold outside."

"Did you have a nice Christmas? I was disappointed that you could not spend it with me."

"Michael could not get away so I offered to work." Amanda shot a look at George who had not said much. "O'ma said you had something of importance to discuss with me. Is Esther all right? I'm afraid . . . with all of my school work . . . I have been very lax in writing to her."

"She still has an occasional nightmare of the flood, but other than that she is functioning normally. Ruth is a good baby, easy to care for. Gail was a real handful when she was a baby. Still is, in fact."

Amanda laughed as she remembered the spunky little girl with a mind of her own. "I hope if Michael and I have a little girl she will be just like Gail."

O'ma looked at her over the top of her glasses. "Are you planning to start a family soon?"

"Not till I finish training."

"Don't put it off too long, child. I assume you are approaching thirty and it's harder to conceive when you are older. Will your husband be able to come to New York later to spend some time with you?"

"If my Uncle Ford can take time away from his farm and go to St. Simons to manage the hotel. We hope he can come for at least a month. That's the plan but nothing is final."

"Where will Michael stay?"

"Hopefully he can find a room that will be close to the Nurses Home. It will be convenient and cheaper."

"Nonsense. I would love to have him here and get to know him. My spare bedroom is available. No one comes to see me in the winter and the days are so short and dreary."

"Oh, but we wouldn't want to impose."

"I would love to have some company." Her eyes twinkled. "You have become like family to me. Now, no arguments. When you know he is coming we will have the room ready. You are free to come and go as your schedule permits."

George cleared his throat. "Esther sends her love. In fact she is planning a family vacation at your resort on St. Simons Island once you are finished with your training and settled. That isn't why I wanted to talk to you. It's about that little boy in Chambersburg I wrote you about. The one with the harelip."

"Bobby Keefer?"

"Yes. In fact that is why I am attending this conference. Several renowned specialists are lecturing on cleft palate and lip repair.

Amanda cocked her head. "How does that involve me?"

"I would like to bring the child to Boston and do the surgery. Chambersburg has no hospital and the work would have to be done at Massachusetts General. I wrote to the home, as you suggested, and they are quite willing to release him to my care. Bobby, I'm afraid is not so willing. He is frightened and suspicious. The matron knows how you befriended him and thought that perhaps you could be of help."

"But I cannot possibly take time off from my training to go to Chambersburg and talk to him."

"I realize that." He grinned. "Remember, I was a medical student once. I know how demanding training is. But perhaps you could write him a letter and encourage him. Tell him what a handsome lad he will be after the surgery."

"I would be glad to do that. When do you want him in Boston?"

"As soon as possible. Dr. Wardill, a surgeon on our staff, is quite proficient in cleft palate repair using the von Langenbeck procedure and he offered to assist me in the surgery in a teaching capacity."

"I'll write to Bobby tomorrow. We'll try to work something out. I certainly owe the young fellow that much. I know he thinks I abandoned him when I didn't return from St. Simons. It is a wonderful thing you are doing, George. It will change his entire life."

Just then the maid arrived to announce that dinner was ready and the rest of the evening passed in pleasant conversation. George made no mention of his personal life and Amanda did not ask.

Sitting before the fire, glancing from time to time down the snow-covered lawns ascending to the Hudson, Amanda read the note she had just received from George. The letter she wrote to Bobby Keefer had been effective. He had arrived in Boston on Tuesday, the twelfth of February, and they operated on Friday. The operation was a success and Bobby was fine. George would send her a photograph when Bobby had healed. He was very proud of his venture into cosmetic surgery and had been highly lauded by his superiors. He added that he was taking the child back to Chambersburg, then going on to Pittsburgh to spend several days with his family.

Amanda sat silently, holding the letter, her conscience some-what assuaged at her abandonment of the boy. But there was also a slight twinge of regret as she thought what her own medical future might have been had she pursued a relationship with George. She had no doubt that he would become a fine surgeon. She pursed her lips. No. These thoughts were unworthy of her. She had made the right decision. Michael was her true love. Her soul mate.

And, only a week later, he arrived for a month's stay. She hadn't realized how much she loved and missed him until she saw him stride down the train platform toward her. Her youthful infatuation had matured into a deep love. Older and wiser now, she also knew that she had been right to seek an identity of her own. She rushed into his arms with a confidence she had not known before.

Michael had never been to New York and at first he couldn't get enough of the city. While she was at school he roamed the streets, visiting museums, art galleries, department stores (he had never been in one), churches and the docks. Everything was new and exciting. And he was staying with O'ma whom he had grown to adore. At night he and Amanda lay in bed, holding each other tightly, as he told her of the day's adventures. But the February dawn came late and darkness fell early. He began to get restless. He was anxious about the resort and longed to get back to work.

"I need to return to the hotel," he said one bleak snowy afternoon. "I have some ideas for some promotional advertising and I would like to plan some summer dances. I don't know just how many reservations we have and I'm sure papa would like to get home to prepare the farm for spring planting."

Amanda didn't object. Her training schedule had grown more demanding and it was difficult to make time for studies while commuting up to O'ma's to spend time with Michael.

He left in early March and Amanda threw herself into her

studies. She was taking an extra course in chemistry, taught by Lavinia Dock. Amanda adored the fiery little woman with her vivid personality and dry wit. Lavinia was working on her second book, *Materia Medica for Nurses*, and had written various articles for medical journals. She had become not only a mentor, but a friend to Amanda. They met often in a little coffee shop near Bellevue where Lavinia brought enthusiasm, humor, and idealism to their lengthy discussions. Lavinia thought doctors were selfish and stupid when they refused to recognize the worth of well-trained nurses and she was not afraid to say so. She was also an active suffragette and never felt the need to moderate her language—which could be quite colorful—or to harness her feeling on issues about women's rights.

April brought the first sure signs of spring with longer days and frequent showers. Whenever Amanda could spare the time she rode the El up to Central Park to walk their lovely paths among leafing trees and blooming tulips. O'ma often joined her on these walks and Amanda had begun to think of her as a surrogate mother.

In May she spent two weeks working in the lying-in ward. She was surprised to find that many of the young mothers were single, several of whom confessed to her that their babies had been sired by fathers or brothers. This was a side of society she knew nothing about. Her naiveté confused and upset her.

June produced a note from George saying that on his way to Pittsburgh he stopped in Chambersburg to check on Bobby. He'd healed well with only a slight scar to his upper lip. Unfortunately Bobby was still belligerent and had not been adopted.

Amanda felt a fresh surge of remorse as she thought about the young boy. At times she still contemplated adopting him but she doubted Michael would be receptive to the idea. He was anxious to start a family of his own.

In July Amanda attended a motivational speech given by

Lavinia about the Henry Street Settlement Lillian Wald was working to establish and the need for visiting nurses to staff it. She stressed the idea that the new field of social work could be satisfying to women of ability for it permitted the development of intellectual, organizational, administrative and executive powers." Lavinia closed her speech with, "The old stiff minds must give way. The old selfish minds must go. The young are at the gates!" Amanda took the message to heart. She was ready to storm a few gates.

Chapter Thirteen

August brought a letter from Michael saying that his father was unable to come south to care for the hotel while he came north for her certification. The hatchery had been sold and although his father was reducing his farm work by not rebuilding the barn, he had twisted his back repairing some roof shingles. So Michael had hired an able young man for the desk and was planning to leave the hotel in his hands for two weeks in September. With two weeks they would have time for that missed honeymoon, he stated, with several exclamation marks.

True to his word, on a brilliant day in mid September, Michael handed the keys to the hotel to his hired hand and directed his carriage through the pillared entrance of the hotel toward the marina. He drove across an island bustling with activity, then through the colored half of town, an area that had never recovered from the hurricane. Children played in grassless yards littered with piles of broken tabby and sand. Cabins leaned and sagged. He passed old women working in their meager gardens. Men of various ages stood in clusters, hand-rolled cigarettes hanging from slack lips. There was an air of hopelessness in the way they moved about—a sense that for them life would never change. In a way the island was much like Charleston, though on a much smaller scale—the division between the very rich and the very poor stark and unsettling. Funny he hadn't noticed that before. Was this what Amanda saw?

•   •   •

Michael arrived in New York on Monday. Amanda would receive her certificate and pin on Thursday at a service with two other young women. As a special surprise he booked a room at the Astor House Hotel on Broadway. After all, this week was also going to be their honeymoon and, he hoped, a new beginning for both of them.

Amanda was thrilled with his choice of the Astor, a great, massive, granite building fronting on Broadway and that evening they had a delicious dinner and several glasses of wine as they talked and talked of the recent past and their future.

That night they lay sated and content snuggled in each others arms. "Do you think maybe we made a baby tonight?" he murmured through half-closed eyes.

"It would be nice. We could name her Aster."

"Her? It will surely be a boy after the vigorous way I claimed you when I finally got you to bed.

Amanda laughed and he kissed the top of her head."

" I met Anson Dodge, rector of Christ Church at Frederica, last week," Michael said. "He came to the hotel to book a room for a friend who pastors the Episcopalian Church here in New York. Did you know Reverend Dodge is building a home for boys in memory of his little boy. It is called The Dodge Home for Boys and it is on the grounds of the old fort on the north end of the island."

I did hear that. The child was killed by a run-away horse, wasn't he?"

"Yes." Michael heaved a deep sigh. "I liked Reverend Dodge. He is a good looking man in his thirties with piercing dark eyes that seem to look right through you. Despite all the tragedy in his life he was very cheerful. The story is that he married his cousin, Ellen, with whom he was very much in love. They left on a honeymoon around the world but Ellen died of a fever in

India. He promised never to leave her so he had her body buried under the pulpit at Christ Church. He married a second time and they had a son. Then, when only three years old, the little boy was killed in that terrible accident. Still, Dodge appeared to have quite a sense of humor and we talked at lenght. He asked me if I would like to serve on the Board of Directors for the Home."

"Oh Michael, how wonderful. You have always been so good with children. I hope you said yes."

"I did."

Amanda turned on her side to face him and looked deep into his eyes. "Speaking of little boys I have been haunted by feelings of failure when I think of young Bobby Keefer."

"Failure? Heavens, Amanda, you were instrumental in getting his lip fixed by that doctor friend of yours."

"I know . . . but . . . but I didn't adopt him."

Michael sat bolt upright in bed. "Adopt! You weren't even married."

"Well I am now."

"Darling you can't be serious. You have more than satisfied your obligation to Bobby. We are planning a family of our own." He reached over and tweaked her nose. "In fact the deed may already be done."

"I guess you are right." She pursed her lips and closed her eyes. "But I still feel guilty about letting him get so attached to me and then just disappearing from his life. I helped him physically but what that child craves is love and a family to belong to. It's what we all want."

Michael lay back on the bed and fell silent. This longing to heal things was typical of Amanda. Over the years he had watched her make a pet of an obnoxious chicken, nurse birds with broken wings, and be a little mother to her baby step-brother. Michael remembered her lecture to him on forgiveness and love. He could use some of her empathy towards others. He frowned, deep in thought. He had always wanted a large family and they were getting a late start. But adopt? Maybe it wasn't so far fetched after all.

He cleared his throat. "Amanda, maybe we could talk to Reverend Dodge about bringing Bobby to the Home. That way you could maintain an active role in his life."

"I don't know if that would be fair to him or make things worse." She smiled tenderly. "But thank you, dear, for understanding. I'm pleased that you will be serving on the board. Maybe I can do a little volunteer nursing there."

"Whatever we do I want it to be together. And speaking of that. . . .

Sunlight was streaming into the hotel room when Michael felt Amanda stir. She snaked an arm across his chest.

"I have to get up," she whispered. "I'm not free yet. I have clinic duty this morning."

He pulled her to him and kissed her. Once, then once again. She giggled and pushed him away. With a groan he let her go and sat on the edge of the bed. As he pulled on his pants she scurried into the bathroom and began to dress.

"Will you meet me at the hospital after lunch so we can go to the Nurses Home and pack?" she called through the open door. "In addition to my regular clothing I have uniforms and a lot of books."

Michael frowned. "How will we transport everything to the hotel?"

"We can hire a lorry. They are all over the city."

"Why don't we pack everything into boxes and ship it to St. Simons. That way we won't be burdened with extra luggage on our way home." He smiled roguishly. "I haven't told you my other surprise. I reserved three nights at a resort hotel in Ocean Grove, New Jersey."

Amanda threw her arms around him. "I love you," she said.

"Um," he mumbled. "And if you get any closer you are definitely going to be late for work."

"Is that a promise?"

"It is."

She pushed him away, playfully. "I'll see you at one o'clock."

Michael spotted Amanda at the reception desk in the Bellevue lobby talking to the receptionist. "Here you are . . ." he was saying, when the wide front door flew open and a tattered little girl came hurtling through. She ran over to them, tears streaming from big blue eyes and grabbed Amanda's blue-and-white-striped uniform skirt with grubby hands. Sobbing incoherently she told Amanda that a baby had been born and her mother wouldn't stop bleeding.

Amanda didn't hesitate. Taking the child's hand she said, "Take me to her." To Michael she called, "Come with us."

The little girl led them across several roadways, between tall, reeking houses with fire escapes bulging with household goods and dirty mattresses. Drizzling rain added to the dismal appearance of the crowded streets, intensifying the nauseous odors. The child pulled Amanda along and they passed evil-smelling, uncovered garbage cans and to Michael's mortification an open truck where a disgusting form of indecency was occurring.

Running, and still crying, the little girl led them through a courtyard, up litter-filled steps into an old walk-up tenement and into the sickroom. Her mother lay on a wretched, straw-filled bed soiled with blood. Michael turned away, bile rising in his stomach. But Amanda went immediately to the woman and knelt on the bloody floor beside her. As Amanda worked to staunch the hemorrhage, a crippled man, who introduced himself as the husband, led Michael to a chair and offered him a cup of tea. Michael was too upset to accept. The apartment seemed to consist of two rooms and he counted five children of various ages, white faced and crying.

"Bring me a length of clean cloth," Amanda called out. "Mind you . . . it must be clean."

A girl of about ten ran over to a battered chest of drawers, thought for a minute then pulled out a petticoat, and carried it over. Amanda immediately tore it into strips and used it as packing. She then asked for a basin of water and tenderly bathed the woman, talking softly to her as she worked.

The tiny apartment with paint peeling from the walls and boards on the windows, though crowded with the belongings of seven people, was not unclean. As Michael talked to the husband he realized the man was sensitive to their condition. Badly crippled, he was probably one of the hundreds begging for alms on the streets.

Amanda placed a fresh length of muslin one of the children found under the woman, then turned and glanced around the room. "Where is the baby?" she asked.

"Here," an older girl answered, pointing to a cardboard box. "I washed him up good."

Amanda picked up the baby and quickly examined him. "You did a good job," she said, smiling at the girl.

The infant began to fuss so Amanda carried him over to the woman and placed him on her breast where he immediately began to suckle. "You'll be all right, now," Amanda assured the mother. "The bleeding has stopped. I won't be here tomorrow but I will have the hospital send a visiting nurse to check you and remove the packing."

The woman reached up and kissed Amanda's hands.

No words were necessary.

Michael held Amanda's arm as they retraced their steps through the tenements in relative silence. As they approached Bellevue he gave his wife a weak smile. "Let's stop at a café. I really need a cup of strong, hot coffee."

While he stirred milk and sugar into his coffee he realized his hand was trembling. This had been a baptism of fire for him. He fixed his gaze on his wife. Amanda was sipping her coffee, her blue eyes calm, her shoulders back. He moved the cup of coffee back and forth. "I never noticed real poverty until today. I . . . I mean . . . really noticed it. I guess I've seen it, yet not seen it. I'll admit it shook me."

"Slums are not only on New York's Lower East Side, Michael. Have you not seen the poverty in the neighborhoods of former slaves on your beautiful island?"

He picked the coffee up, then set it down. "I guess I just didn't pay much attention."

"I've gotten used to it on the wards. You know, Michael, all the muddled aspects of the social and economic relations in this country were represented in our journey today. You and I were fortunate enough to be born into families with the means to educate and give us a respectable standard of living. What chance does that child have who was born today in the slums of New York?"

Amanda looked strong and confident and abruptly Michael recognized the path their lives had taken. She had a calling. She needed to be her own person. She was a woman of great complexity—a woman who knew her own heart and who had responded to today's emergency with purpose and self-confidence.

He understood now. And he loved her even more for it. But he was troubled. Amanda had opened a door that had taken him into her world. And her world was beyond the confines of McKenzie Resort. He had wanted her to fit into his arena but now he knew—really knew—it would never be enough to make her happy. He toyed with his spoon, stirring the cooling coffee. He remembered the colored neighborhood he had driven through on his way to the marina. Amanda had often mentioned a desire to do social work. Perhaps she could improve the living conditions of the former slaves; maybe she would start a small clinic on the island. He smiled to himself as his spirits lifted and he realized that he was ready, not just to accept this path his wife had chosen, but to help her in any way possible. Michael felt a stir of excitement. It was time to enter a world new and challenging for both of them. With a surge of elation he jumped up, spilling half the contents of his cup into his saucer. "Come on," he cried to a startled Amanda. "We both have a goal. I'm with you, sweetheart. At last I see the light. I've been looking for you to help me. I want to help you. I know it will be hard and I will probably get frustrated sometimes. Maybe even angry at your independence and things I can't change. But I think I can grow along with you." Amanda rose to meet him and he pulled her into his arms. He tilted her chin and gazed into her eyes.

"Today is the day we start our new life together," he said softly.

The End

Author's Note

This book is a work of historical fiction based on real people and real events.

I have tried to be factually accurate in telling this story. In 1882 gas lights were still in use in Chambersburg, Pennsylvania. Horse cars were still really running in New York City in the 1880s and the *arm* of the Statue of Liberty did stand in Madison Square until funds were raised to erect the pedestal on Ellis Island.

I have, however, taken advantage of an author's license to occasionally adjust the timeline to fit the story. The fine old Dakota apartment building which I depict in 1882 wasn't actually finished until 1885, The Dodge Home for Boys, and Wolf Park opened several years after the end of my story. So there are some deliberate inaccuracies, but then this is only a story, offered as entertainment.

Women, by the 1880s, had made promising gains in higher education but many graduates echoed Amanda's sentiments that educated women had few outlets for their training and were left adrift, their schooling frequently causing them to feel more alienated by their stereotyped roles than before. As a rule a college-educated woman still waited for marriage, feeling frustrated because of an inability to deploy talents she was not actually sure she possessed. This is the theme I have endeavored to develop.

Lavinia Dock (1858-1956) was a real person—an educator, settlement worker, author, pacifist and suffragist who strove to improve the public health movement while continually elevating the status of women. And she had a connection with Chambersburg, Pennsylvania.

Born into a prosperous family in Harrisburg, Pennsylvania, she chose to train as a nurse at New York City's Bellevue Hospital, later serving as a visiting nurse among the poor. She and her sisters retired to the Caledonia area east of Chambersburg in 1922. Their home was located off Route 30 beside the old Graeffenburg Inn. Her contribution to the field of nursing— which helped transform what was then a despised trade into a genuine scientific profession—earned her recognition as an architect of modern nursing. Her *Materia Medica for Nurses* (1890) is still the standard work on that subject. Her other books on nursing are among the textbooks used in most modern schools.

When the dam above Johnstown, Pennsylvania collapsed Miss Dock was among the first nurses to arrive in the ravaged valley. Six months later she returned to New York as night supervisor at Bellevue and later served at Johns Hopkins in Baltimore. Although she gave up nursing at the age of fifty and retired to the Dock home at Caledonia she dedicated her energies to outspoken activism on controversial social issues of the day, such as the elimination of prostitution and venereal diseases, and women's rights. She spoke out against World War I and was an early advocate of birth control. She is known to have lectured both at Wilson College and at the Graeffenburg Inn, which appears to have been suffrage headquarters.

Mira Dock, Lavinia's older sister, was a renown botanist and enjoyed an outstanding career in forestry and town planning. She collected pine seeds from all over the world and grew the seedlings on their land at Caledonia. These young trees were later moved to land now located at the Penn State campus in Mt.

Alto. Mira was a writer, lecturer, lobbyist and authority of national and international reputation on tree identification and conservation practices.

The system of public health nursing, or social work as we know it today, was started by Miss Lillian Wald. While a young student at Bellevue she became aware of the problems of the residents of the city's Lower East Side and of the intolerable but little-known conditions in which they lived. In the late 1800s friends provided her with a building for her work and the Henry Street Settlement, a tenement clinic treating the ill and teaching sanitation and hygiene, was born.

Hospitals in their early years combined the city poorhouse, the house of correction, and hospital wards all in one, staffed with uneducated nurses some of whom were short-term prisoners. Then, a group of women led by Louisa Lee Schuyler formed the Bellevue Hospital Visiting Committee. This committee visited the wards and from what they learned grew the determination to train proper nurses.

My dialogue between Mrs. Schuyler and O'ma was taken from an actual report of the Bellevue Visiting Committee which ended with the phrase: "The nurses were prisoners arrested for drunkenness, immorality, or other misdemeanors, who slept in the bath-rooms on straw beds, terrorized the helpless sick, took bribes, and were not to be trusted with medicines nor with food brought in by visitors."

We have certainly come a long way.

Georgia often escapes major hurricanes because its coastline is nestled in a protective indentation. Hurricanes moving south to north jump from Jacksonville, Florida, to the next-largest land mass jutting into the Atlantic, Cape Hatteras, North Carolina The last major hurricane to hit St. Simons, the one depicted in this book, killed over one hundred people. A few deaths have been blamed on hurricanes that have brushed Georgia since the late 1800s but some experts say they were not directly caused by the storms.

The Johnstown Flood will go down in the annals of history as one of worst national disasters in American history. There were many reasons why the dam collapsed: lowering of the crest when the original dam was repaired by non-skilled workers, the use of debris instead of mortar to build the dam, the failure to install any outlet pipes at its base. As the water rose, stumps, logs, underbrush and whole trees jammed the artificial iron fish screens in the spillway, installed by the rich members of the South Fork Hunting and Fishing Club to protect their sport.

Of specific interest to Chambersburg, a real town in south-central Pennsylvania, I offer the following:

The Children's Aid Society of Franklin County was organized in 1884 in response to state legislation mandating that children between the ages of two and sixteen could not be kept in poorhouses longer than sixty days. The first home in Chambersburg was opened at 148 E. King Street, then moved to Chambersburg's East Point, and again to South Franklin Street. In 1886 it was moved to Federal Hill on North Franklin Street at Pleasant Street. That house was razed in 1976 when Doctor and Mrs. Benjamin F. Myers Memorial Home opened. It is still operating.

The Chambersburg Hospital and the Shook Home were both founded by the Children's Aid Society. When the society was first formed the nearest hospital to Chambersburg was in Harrisburg. In 1889 the Society's board began a campaign to start a hospital and in 1895 they opened a hospital in a converted home at 217 S. Main Street. In 1904 the hospital was moved to its current home on Lincoln Way East.

To meet the care of adults, the Society opened a home for the aged, which later became the John H. Shook Home for the Aged.

John G. Orr, a character in my book, was a newspaperman and president of the Children's Aid who dedicated forty years to the establishment of both homes and the hospital.

Mrs. Morrow's home is located at 1038 Edgar Avenue. It was built in 1860 by Calvin Mark Duncan, a local attorney, on property owned by Wilson College. In the early 1900s it was rented by Wilson College alumnae and operated as The College Inn, a popular tea room for eight years. It has passed through numerous owners—Morrow, Sharpe, Pomeroy, Mahon, Wood, Strite, Fraver, Shields—and is currently owned by Mr. And Mrs. William Gardner.

Bibliography

History of the Johnstown Flood by Willis Fletcher Johnson. Edgewood Publishing: 1889.

Sudden Sea: The Great Hurricane by R. A. Scotta. Chapter & Verse Ink: 2003.

Three Rivers Rising by Jane Richards. Alfred A. Knopf: 2010.

Johnstown Flood by David McCullough. Simon & Shuster: 1968.

The Great Hurricane 1938 by Cherie Burns. Grove Press: 2005.

About the Author

Dody Myers is the author of one contemporary and five historical novels. Once again with ONLY ECHOES REMAIN, the third of the Echoes Saga, she blends historical fact and real people with fictional characters to put a human face on our past.

She divides her time between Chambersburg, Pennsylvania and St. Simons Island, Georgia.

CPSIA information can be obtained
at www.ICGtesting.com
Printed in the USA
BVHW03s0943070318
509878BV00001B/4/P